IMAGINE IF YOU WILL that the BFI had a disreputable cousin, a Northern Grindhouse with tastes a little darker and stranger. With staff who love their movies with a passion that borders on religious zeal, who know you by name and welcome you in as they throw the doors open at midnight. Whose programming runs the gamut of worldwide genre film making, praising the strange, the unusual, the weird and forgotten.

SOUNDS GOOD?

Then step inside the **ELECTRIC DREAMHOUSE**! A new cinema imprint from PS Publishing and Editor Neil Snowdon . . .

Settle down and get comfortable as we raise the curtain on our 'MIDNIGHT MOVIE MONOGRAPHS' — an ongoing series dedicated to outstanding genre titles that just don't get the attention elsewhere.

Written by genre authors, film makers and some of the finest critical voices on the scene, bringing a unique perspective to films they love, these are not dry academic texts. They are passionate, incisive, and inspiring explorations that go deep, from writers who know and love the genre inside out. Expert — indeed award winning — practitioners in their field.

Intelligent, accessible film writing is part of what keeps the subject fresh, vital, alive. In recent years it seems to have fallen through the cracks a bit. It's still there, but you have to go looking. Academic Film Studies and the 'Cultural Elite' have built linguistic walls of arid language around our favourite films, while Mainstream Media speak mostly in sound-bites and exclamation marks.

Film is a universal language. A synthesis of all the great Arts, with the ability to speak across boundaries of class, race and age to move us, inspire us, illuminate our deepest fears.

Film is Art with a capital A, but none of the social and cultural snobbery that implies. Film writing should be the same.

Passionate. Incisive. Intelligent. Accessible. These are our watch words.

ROLL FILM

MIDNIGHT MOVIE MONOGRAPHS

MARTIN

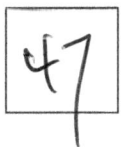

This first edition of **MARTIN**
is limited to 500 copies
of which this copy is

47

MIDNIGHT MOVIE MONOGRAPHS

JEZ WINSHIP

To Neil, who made it all happen.
Thanks for inviting me over the threshold.

MARTIN (1977) is a film which stands out as a singular work within the oeuvre of writer and director George A Romero and he has long cited it as his personal favourite. Its quietude and reflective, melancholy tone are in marked contrast to the violent, confrontational nature of the new breed of independent American horror movies which appeared in the 1970s. If **EASY RIDER** (1969) was the foundation film, the ur-movie for the new wave re-energising the moribund output of the big studios, then **NIGHT OF THE LIVING DEAD** (1968) was the parallel exemplar for the new generation of young horror directors (although Roger Corman also played his part in giving film-makers in both camps a valuable and practically-minded apprenticeship). Pictures like **THE TEXAS CHAINSAW MASSACRE** (1974), **LAST HOUSE ON THE LEFT** (1972) and **THE HILLS HAVE EYES** (1977) were characterised by a brutal, unflinching realism and raw savagery which mirrored the violent tenor of the times and the seismic social ructions causing division across the country, amongst families and between the generations. The post-countercultural era of Nixon, Watergate and its fall-out of political disaffection and widespread paranoia was also marked by the continued attrition of the Vietnam war and the final concession by the US government of its intractability, the increasing prominence of identity politics in terms of gender, race and sexuality, and the steady decline of the economy, with all the attendant hardships and social ills. **MARTIN** addresses such issues, but views them from an oblique angle, its social observations embedded in what is, at heart, a deeply affecting study of an alienated, withdrawn and lonely young man.

I first encountered the film during an all-night George Romero programme at the legendary Scala Cinema in London in the 1980s. I'd seen Romero's three zombie films to date, as well as **THE CRAZIES** (1973), something of a staple of BBC Saturday night horror double bills. I was eager to add **MARTIN** to my list. Watching it in a semi-conscious state of drift in the early hours of the morning, its air of sadness and quiet desolation had a profound effect upon me. John Amplas' embodiment of the character of Martin in particular left a very strong impression. A video recording from the TV became an oft-viewed treasure, punctuated with the tiny ellisions caused by the heavy clunk of the stop button on a chunky, top-loading VCR. It was one of those films which defined my adolescence and young adulthood, whose scenes, music and dialogue were indelibly imprinted on my impressionable brain. I have revisited it many times in the succeeding years, its familiarity and sustained emotional resonance creating a direct connection with those long-gone days, whilst also finding new levels of consonance with my current state and situation at the time of viewing.

It's a film which invites such a personal relationship. But it is also a fine study of a particular time and place, of the way in which both social and familial environments affect the individual and the community at large. There is a great deal going on in **MARTIN**. It works on a multitude of levels without ever descending into laboured didacticism or heavily under-lined symbolism. The opportunity to have a really close look at this film which has meant so much to me over the years, to study its manifold layers, is both irresistible and slightly intimidating. Picking apart a work of art you love risks dissipating its magic. You will also, inevitably, uncover something of yourself in the process, discover what it is about the film which draws you to it, reveal potentially unknown corners of your soul. But let us cast all doubts aside and proceed. Climb on board that night train to Pittsburgh . . .

The film begins with a departure, a guard calling "all aboard", something of an invitation to the audience. There is an immediate sense that the film we are about to see is part of a larger narrative whole. We are about to embark for the setting of the next episode, to start at a chapter significantly removed from the beginning of the story. What happened *before* is, and will perhaps remain, something of a mystery.

In a work which self-consciously draws on the vampire mythos and the representation of the vampire on the page and, most markedly, in the cinema, this opening journey could be seen as echoing the migration of Dracula in Bram Stoker's novel. Stoker's aristocratic count travels from the peasant society of the old world on the eastern fringes of Europe to the modern, steam-driven, metropolitan heart of the Victorian empire, London; the thriving, densely populated centre of its financial and trade networks. Martin's journey takes him from an old world, dimly alluded to at various points (although it appears to be Indianapolis, as we later discover) to the declining industrial city of Braddock, near Pittsburgh. If London was full of fresh blood, the lifeforce of a thriving imperial power with, by implication, the pulsing throb of economic vitality to feed upon, the Braddock to which Martin travels has already been drained dry[1]. The comparison is the first of many more or less explicit instances in which Romero deromanticises elements of the old mythos, recasting them in a modern, realistic form. Blowing away the mist and dynamiting the crumbling, ruinous castles.

---

[1] Braddock was the perfect setting for such a realist fable. A satellite town on the Monongahela River a few miles beyond Pittsburgh, it was one of the first places in what was to become the north-eastern manufacturing belt of the US to be transformed by a thoroughgoing process of industrialisation. Andrew Carnegie built his first steel mill here in 1875, the Edgar Thompson Steel Works, so the town can be seen as the foundation of one of the great accumulations of personal wealth in the late 19th and early 20th centuries; the American dream writ large. It was also the site of the first Carnegie public library, built in 1889, a public endowment which was also a tactical public relations gesture. Carnegie certainly had need of such gestures to allay discontents arising from his robust attitude towards labour relations. The nearby Homestead steel plant, which he also owned, was the site of one of the great confrontations in the history of the American labour movement. The Amalgamated Association of Iron and Steel Workers had fought for fair wages and decent working conditions, and Carnegie decided that it was time to break their power. He refused to renew the collective bargaining agreements with the union and, via his deputy Henry Clay Frick, imposed a significant wage decrease. To break the resultant strike and picket of the plant, 300 Pinkerton agents were hired and a pitched battle took place on July 5th 1892, with several casualties on both sides. The Pennsylvania state militia was called out and when they arrived they sided with the Pinkertons and the steel mill owners. It became clear where the real power lay. The union was effectively broken.

We initially have an insider's viewpoint, looking out from the vestibule of the train, the open doorway framing the platform outside. We watch a woman climb on board (the ascent seems fairly steep from the perspective of a British train traveller) whilst another waits outside. And then Martin appears, effortfully heaving his cumbersome bag up the steps. He looks back at the woman on the platform, hesitating on the threshold. This is the first of a good many scenes in which we see Martin lingering on some threshold. These scenes play upon the lore of the vampire having to be invited in to the domestic space. As with all the elements of vampire lore which Romero confronts in the film, there is a rational explanation which overwrites the supernatural. Any hesitancy in Martin's case is an adjunct of personality rather than inherent devilry (although, as we shall see, the line between the two can become blurred). He is pathologically shy and withdrawn and wouldn't consider crossing the threshold of someone's household unless unequivocally invited in. Even then, he'd practically have to be dragged through the door. Of course, his surreptitious house invasions are a different matter. Here, at the beginning, the call of the train guard acts as a general invitation.

As John Amplas makes his appearance as the title character, we see the words "A Laurel Presentation" on the screen. This is a highly significant pronouncement, heralding the beginning of a new collaborative endeavour which would prove a success on a creative, business and personal level. The combination of the three elements have always seemed essential to Romero's working practices. He would rather not work at all than dispense with any of them. His first four films had been made under the banner of the Latent Image production company, which Romero and various compatriots had set up in Pittsburgh in 1963. They had set out to establish themselves as a viable commercial force by making TV ads and industrial promotion films. Always in the back of their minds, however, was the ultimate goal of making a feature length picture. In 1967, they decided the time was right, and a group of ten friends from Latent Image decided to invest their own money to get the project started. And so, **NIGHT OF THE LIVING DEAD** was produced by the Image Ten group, with further investment coming from local Pittsburgh businesses. The collective spirit behind the making of the picture proved frustrating in practical terms. The distribution deal with Continental, part of the Walter Reade Organisation, resulted in much bitterness and litigation in the wake of the film's steadily accumulating cult status and critical reputation, and the wholly unanticipated degree of its financial success.

Romero tried to move away from the horror genre in his next three films, approaching it tangentially if at all. THERE'S ALWAYS VANILLA (1971) was a kooky comedy in the mould of THE GRADUATE (1967), with some pointed and at times uncomfortable observations about the prevailing culture, whether straight or counter; JACK'S WIFE (1972) (aka SEASON OF THE WITCH, allowing for Donovan's song to be superimposed on the soundtrack) was a drama adopting the subjective viewpoint of a middle-aged suburban housewife dabbling in witchcraft which reflected the impact of the burgeoning women's liberation movement and again took a questioning approach to its material; and THE CRAZIES was a satirical, anti-establishment action picture in which chaos descends on a small town in the wake of a biological weapon spillage and local citizens take up arms against a chaotically run army sent by a panicked government to impose martial law.

Romero honed his directorial and editorial craft on these films, as well as learning hard lessons about the business of moviemaking. They met with a mixed critical reception when they were noticed at all, and none of them were financially successful. With Latent Image straining under heavy debts, a new direction was desperately needed.

Cometh the hour, cometh the man. As if magically summoned, Richard Rubinstein arrived on the scene. He interviewed Romero for a film magazine at the time THE CRAZIES was being released. But what he really wanted was to get into the business side of the film industry. He and Romero hit it off, and they decided to set up their own independent company, which they named Laurel. Romero had previously established Laurel Tape and Film as a potential business vehicle, but had yet to actually use it. Laurel produced a number of successful sports documentaries for television between 1973–76 (including one on OJ Simpson in the year of his greatest triumph) which, along with a number of other ventures (importing foreign films and book publishing amongst them) set it on a sufficiently firm financial footing to be able to contemplate making its first feature. A group of local Pittsburgh business investors were found willing to stump up $100,000. Romero took a pre-existing idea and developed it with the budgetary restrictions in mind. **MARTIN** was born. A new start, a new train, a new direction.

A shot of the tracks lit up by the train's locomotive lantern gives an impressionistic sense of the journey's progress, the silvery curves of the rail like a moonlit sketch of a river's winding course. The title MARTIN is superimposed, as if it too is illuminated by the train's light, caught in its bright glare. It's at this point that the first notes of Donald Rubinstein's score sound, a descending minor key chord sequence voiced with the appropriately silvery, mercurially reverberant tones of the electric piano. Over the top, a vibraphone plays a sad, lyrical theme, the sort of yearning melody Ornette Coleman used to come up with in pieces such as Lonely Woman.

The electric piano was an instrument popular with jazz fusioneers of the 70s, its use underlines the jazz foundations of Rubinstein's music. In this sense, it bears comparison with Kryzytof Komeda's score for Roman Polanski's 1967 film **DANCE OF THE VAMPIRES**, another vampire

8

movie soundtrack with jazz shadings (heard mainly in the bass lines in this instance). Both also use melodic flute for some of the lighter interludes. The initial chord sequence, a slow, mournful cascade full of melancholic resignation and lonely, late night reflection, combined with the sorrowful melody, recurs at various points of the film in differing arrangement and effectively constitutes **MARTIN**'s theme. It's about as far as you could get from James Bernard's strident orchestral chords pronouncing the syllables of Dra-cu-la at the beginning of the 1958 Hammer film.[2]

Martin sits alone at a dimly illuminated table, playing a game of solitaire, his solitude immediately established. Low, heavily phased notes, unstable and dizzying, create a mood of brooding menace. He shuffles the cards and places them in the pack, ready for action, switching off the light as he leaves. In the corridor of the sleeper compartment, its red-curtained cubicles stacked in two-tiered rows like sepulchres in an old cemetery, an arm protrudes limply out into the narrow space. Martin edges past, looking nervous and anxious not to wake any of the snoring sleepers. It's a scene which brings to mind the night corridors negotiated by characters in Roman Polanski's **REPULSION** (1965) and Val Lewton's **BEDLAM** (1946), both of which sprout sudden thickets of grasping hands. In utter contrast, it also recalls Jack Lemmon's furtive nocturnal excursions to Marilyn Monroe's cubicle in **SOME LIKE IT HOT** (1959). This is the first of many confining spaces in which Martin is placed, restrictive interiors which symbolically reflect the straitened circumstances of his existence.

He edges forward with a khaki bag held out before him, protective of its contents. A soft, bundled baggage, it looks like the traditional vampire

---

[2] In his sleeve notes to the Ship to Shore records repressing of his soundtrack, Donald Rubinstein recalls how he composed the score in his flat in Watertown, Massachussetts based solely on his reading of Romero's script. 'It was so good and all I needed', he wrote. It was an intensely concentrated period of creative endeavour in which he wholly lost himself in the work for several months. 'I was really working on instinct', he comments in Paul R. Gagne's book THE ZOMBIES THAT ATE PITTSBURGH. He took some of his initial recordings down to Pittsburgh, and received an overwhelmingly positive response from Romero and cinematographer Michael Gornick (who declared it to be 'perfect'). Encouraged, he returned to finish the score. In the documentary included in the Arrow Films Special Edition DVD of **MARTIN**, he notes that some parts were later written to film. Romero also mentions on the commentary that some scenes were cut to the rhythms of the music in the editing room. It really is an essential component of the film's overall affect.

hunter's kit bag, ready to be swiftly unrolled when the call to action arrives, a selection of sharpened stakes and sturdy wooden mallet immediately to hand. Martin enters the confined space of the toilet. From a practical point of view, it's worth noting that all of these scenes were filmed on board a real, if stationary train in a siding of Pittsburgh station. Of necessity, the work was done when the daily timetable was in slumbering abeyance. There must have been some very intimate huddles during this part of the shoot. If crew and actors weren't closely acquainted with each other before, they certainly would have been by the time these night shoots were wrapped up.

Martin's preparations in the toilet add a further element of deromanticisation. Toilets and bathrooms feature as recurrent locales in the film, and act as a persistent reminder of the physicality of the human body and its biological processes (and there's no greater leveller than a reminder of our common excretory functions). This effectively dispels the disembodied enchantments of the supernatural, of the vampire's remote, mesmeric powers of seduction. Romero's horror films in general have rejected the supernatural for the bodily. They have always been grounded in a pronounced physicality, most obviously in the flesh rending and devouring of the living dead films. Although the word zombie is never uttered in those films, they have effectively reinvented the canonical monster raised from the dead by Voodoo invocation. Once more, the supernatural is cast aside in favour of a more corporeal horror. In Romero's third film, **JACK'S WIFE/SEASON OF THE WITCH,** Joan's venture into the practice of magic and supernatural charms, her progress towards becoming a witch, is viewed with scepticism. Rather than a move towards liberation and self-assertion, it is presented as a retreat into compensatory self-delusion; a path offering an illusory sense of empowerment. Romero is at heart a realist. This is the central thesis of Tony Williams' book THE CINEMA OF GEORGE ROMERO: KNIGHT OF THE LIVING DEAD, complete with high-minded allusions to the novels of Emil Zola; a comparison which would no doubt amuse the self-effacing and down-to-earth director.

Martin looks more relaxed now that he is on his own, locked away in this small, sepulchral space. A glance back with open mouth gives us a flash of Amplas' incisors, a slight gap between them giving a vague hint of Max Schreck or Klaus Kinski's Nosferatu in his youth (appropriate given the repeated use of the description as a form of curse later on). John Amplas conveys profound depths of nuanced feeling through his gazes, glances and sideways looks throughout the film. Martin is a watcher, an observer hiding away in the peripheral shadows, never taking centre stage but waiting in the wings, gauging the performance of those around him. Amplas himself never got the big roles, the parts which would have showcased the talents he displayed in **MARTIN**. Romero still expresses regrets over this to this day and proselytises over his acting abilities in an interview given to Lee Karr for the *Homepage of the Dead* website in 2009: "I thought John was the most talented actor I'd ever seen and a particularly angelic sort of type... I don't know why John never made it, but I think if the right guy had seen John, he would have been..." Romero never finishes the sentence, but you can tell he is thinking 'one of the greats'.

Amplas had small roles in most of Romero's films made for Laurel, but they often seemed to be deliberately disguised, as if he were trying to efface his presence. In **DAWN OF THE DEAD** (1978), he is one of the armed Puerto Ricans fighting back against the S.W.A.T team invading their tenement at the start of the film, and is all but unrecognisable with Che beard and moustache, long hair held back by a revolutionary bandana. In **KNIGHTRIDERS** (1981), he has a silent role as a jester in Ed Harris' noble Arthurian biker court, his face obscured by a mime's white paint throughout. In **CREEPSHOW** (1982), he is entirely enshrouded in the rotting corpse make-up of the revolting, re-animated Nathan in the 'Father's Day' segment of the film, but essays a classic shuffling, swaying zombie walk. In **DAY OF THE DEAD** (1985), he is one of the still, small voices of reason in the purgatorial bunker presided over by bullish military and inhumane scientific powers, and is gunned down in a brutal assertion of martial authority. Amplas has had a few other film roles, but he has stayed true to his roots and acted in, produced and directed a good many acclaimed productions at the Pittsburgh Playhouse where Romero first saw him. Happily, he is also passing on his wisdom and experience to future generations of actors having taught at the Conservatory of Performing Arts at Point Park University for a good many years.

Amplas expresses volumes with minimal means; not just in his facial expressions (and the downcast turn of his mouth can be absolutely heartbreaking) but in the way he holds his head, the gestural language of his body, the tension of his posture. In its own restrained way, it's a very physical performance, one which at times resurrects the performance styles of the silent movie era, and at others is filled with a balletic grace of movement.

Like so many of the cast and crew on **MARTIN**, Amplas was discovered by Romero in the environs of Pittsburgh, appearing in a theatrical production of PHILOMEN, a 1975 musical by Tom Jones (no, not that one) and Harvey Schmidt about a Christian martyr in the Roman empire of the 3rd century. He made a deep impression on Romero, and the role of Martin developed to allow him to make the part his own. In Paul R. Gagne's study of Romero's films THE ZOMBIES THAT ATE PITTSBURGH (still the definitive book on the director), Amplas suggests that "as I understand it, for the first couple of drafts, he had been considering somewhat of an older character for the role". Amplas' youthful looks (although he was actually 27 at the time of filming) gave the film an entirely different direction, transforming its emphasis to a significant degree. One of the levels upon which the multi-layered story operates is as a tale of generational conflict, a significant strand in post-60s cinema (and, remembering iconic performances by Brando and Dean, in the youth-oriented cinema of the 50s too).

Amplas became part of the Laurel 'family', the kind of small, closely-knit team which Romero prefers to work with. On the documentary included with the Special Edition DVD, the making of the film is referred to as being 'a family affair'. The sense of a collective creative endeavour which Romero is happiest fostering, means that everyone is emotionally invested in the making of the movie and prepared to lend a hand whenever they can, in whatever capacity. The familial atmosphere was enhanced in this instance by the fact that Romero was at this point dating Christine Forrest, who plays Christina, and whom he would later marry. A lot of the filming took place in the house of local Braddock filmmaker Tony Buba and his brother Pat (or Pasquale, as he is more formally identified in the credits), presided over by their grandmother, who cooked substantial meals for communal feasts.[3]

DVD commentaries and documentary reminiscences all point to the experience as having been a highly pleasurable and creatively inspiring one for all concerned. The making of **MARTIN** was a blessed time, one of those rare periods when everyone is working towards a shared end with a commonality of purpose and enthusiasm. It's the ideal which the courtiers of the latterday King Arthur are working towards in **KNIGHTRIDERS**, a film which is in many ways a fable about collective creative endeavour.

We now get a series of swiftly edited close-up shots of Martin's unrolled bundle. Plastic pockets reflect the stark, comfortless glare of the overhead strip light. There are tight close-ups on a medical phial, a syringe plunger being drawn up and a needle with a drop of the solution it's just sucked up hanging suspended from its stinging tip (a prick — highly phallic if you

---

[3] Tony Buba is something of a Braddock cultural hero. He has been making films in the town since his 1974 short J.Roy: New and Used Furniture. Pictures such as **BETTY'S CORNER CAFÉ** (1976), **SWEET SAL** (1979), **VOICES FROM A STEELTOWN** (1983), **STRUGGLES IN STEEL: THE FIGHT FOR EQUAL OPPORTUNITY** (1996) and his latest, **WE ARE ALIVE: THE FIGHT TO SAVE BRADDOCK HOSPITAL** (2012) have shown a sustained commitment to documenting the town and actively agitating for change. He would undoubtedly have proved an invaluable source of local information and he became a part of Romero's creative family, working on the sound for **MARTIN, DAWN OF THE DEAD** and **DAY OF THE DEAD**, as an assistant editor on **KNIGHTRIDERS**, and taking small roles in **MARTIN** and **DAWN**. Pasquale 'Pat' Buba (who also appears with his brother in **MARTIN**), later became an editor on Romero pictures and would perform that role from **KNIGHTRIDERS** in 1981, until **THE DARK HALF** in 1993. He continues to work with some of the best in the business as part of the editorial team on Martin Scorsese's films **CASINO** (1995) and **GANGS OF NEW YORK** (2002) and for Michael Mann on **HEAT** (1995).

13

choose to view things through a Freudian lens). Romero's editing captures Martin's preparations with the utmost clarity and concision, the fastcut rhythms creating a sense of urgency and anticipation. The practiced control and reflexive efficiency with which he performs these actions makes it clear that this is something which Martin has done on many previous occasions. It's all very clinical, lit with a surgical light which banishes shadows and exposes the clean plastic and steel materials to a disinfecting white radiation. It is the opposite of the romantically suggestive glow of candlelight more common to gothic cinema, whose wavering glow, together with the tenebrous borders beyond the limited compass of its illumination, leaves plenty to the play of the imagination. This fluorescent train toilet glare is the lighting of unsparing realism, stripping away any scope for romantic fantasy.

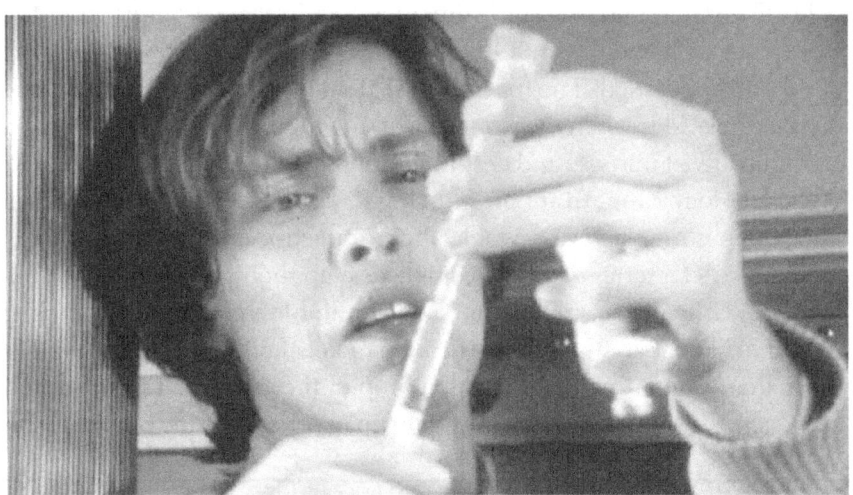

Out in the corridor, Martin puts the syringe in his mouth in order to take his lock-picking tools out and put them to work on the door of the compartment he has earlier noted the lone woman from the platform being ushered into. These are his fangs; clasped between his teeth, the drug-filled syringe chamber and the straight, needle-sharp stinger are like the extended canines of the traditional vampire which force the mouth open into a narrow gape expressing a salivating mixture of hunger and desire. On the soundtrack, the steady beat of drums and rattling percussion, trailing echoed exhalations, summons up the thud of the adrenalin-quickened heart, the increase in the rate of respiration and the jangle of agitated nerves.

As Martin opens the door, we cut from colour to black and white. The contrast of colour and black and white sequences is one of the central stylistic devices of the film. Like similar uses of such contrast in **THE WIZARD OF OZ** (1939), **A MATTER OF LIFE AND DEATH** (1946) AND **STALKER** (1979), it is used to highlight the division between worlds; between dreams, memories and fantasies and directly experienced reality. Martin's fantasies draw on the iconography of the gothic horror film. They may be cast in Universal black and white, but their style is far more redolent of the Hammer films of the 60s and 70s. The softness of the black and white grain, particularly when contrasted with the lighting of the train, suggests a film being projected in Martin's imagination. A woman with long dark hair, dressed in a diaphanous white nightgown, turns around with an inviting look. She is every inch the female archetype from a Hammer vampire movie, from Carol Marsh in **DRACULA** (1958) (aka **HORROR OF DRACULA**) through to Mary Collinson in **TWINS OF EVIL** (1971) (one of the last to be set in the traditional 19th century gothic milieu). We are immediately drawn back from this fantasy however.

We are back in the corridor and the door to the compartment is still closed. Romero's editing creates a jarring disjunction between fantasy and reality, and makes clear the degree to which Martin's imagination impinges upon his perception of reality. The act is restaged, having first been played out on the screen of his mind.

This time when the door is opened, the camera makes a swift sweep of the room, effectively a point of view survey following Martin's assessing scan. This is an atypical use of camera movement by Romero, who preferred at this stage to create movement and pace through editing. The room is empty, but the objects which are picked out all say something about its occupant. They are like a quick, in the moment character sketch. A paperback and newspaper are lying on the bed, reading matter either just put down or ready to be picked up. A small travelling case is open to reveal a box of chocolates, comfort food for a long, lonely journey (we've earlier heard her telling the guard she is travelling alone to New York). Make-up is scattered haphazardly, the mysteries of glamour unceremoniously laid out.

The title of the paperback, which DVD freeze-framing allows us to pick out, is of particular interest. It is BEYOND FREEDOM AND DIGNITY by B.F. Skinner. Skinner was a controversial figure who was instrumental in developing the field of behavioural science, which he characterised as 'a technology of human behaviour'. BEYOND FREEDOM AND DIGNITY, first published in 1971, was a popular summation of the deterministic philosophy of behaviouralism and was a surprise best-seller. Skinner goes beyond notions of freedom and dignity, defining human individualism by denying the individual agency of human behaviour altogether. Humans are not possessed of free will, he claimed (but what impulse drove him to make this claim, then?) and the dignity which might be defined as the recognition of and praise for individually autonomous behaviours and actions is of no value if free will is thus dismissed. His chilling use of phrases such as 'operant conditioning' underlines a disturbingly authoritarian dimension to his philosophy or 'science' of human behaviour. The 'operant' is a human being viewed in terms of an organism programmable through a behavioural science of positive or negative reinforcement, the 'technology of human behaviour'. If human beings and their actions are wholly determined by their environment and the responses they receive from social bodies and authorities, then they can be effectively controlled, their behaviours moulded through rationally applied scientific means. People would be happier being guided by such controls, Skinner believed. The burden of false notions of freedom and individuality would be lifted from them. There is something redolent of THE PRISONER TV series about such ideas. Skinner wrote a utopian novel called WALDEN TWO in which his theories were applied to an isolated community and all social problems were thereby eliminated, allowing all to live the good life. Of course, as with most 'utopias', it is easy to invert the model and recalibrate it in dystopian terms. The presumption that an enlightened and wholly rational scientific priesthood would show the way, guiding 'operants' towards correct behaviour is dubious at best.

MARTIN is informed by Skinnerian ideas in its questioning of the extent to which Martin's behaviour, his quasi-vampiric cravings, are inherent or the result of environmental conditioning. In his highly perceptive afterword to the novelisation of the film, Romero notes that 'to categorise monsters is to expect them to act predictably', reducing them to the level of assimilable and programmable beings (soft machines) as envisaged by Skinner.

Given that Martin's environment is predominantly that of the family, it would not be surprising to find another popular psychology paperback tucked away in the travelling case by the foot of the bed: RD Laing's THE POLITICS OF THE FAMILY (1969), a reiteration of his 1964 book SANITY, MADNESS AND THE FAMILY in which he discerns symptoms of schizophrenia, of the alienation of the self, developing from internalised patterns of behaviour imposed by traditional family structures and conflicting relationships. This certainly Seems germane to Martin's condition, the 'family curse' re-imagined in the modern language of psychiatry rather than being ascribed to an ancient inheritance of spiritual evil. Peter Watson, in his encyclopedic volume A TERRIBLE BEAUTY: A HISTORY OF THE PEOPLE AND IDEAS THAT SHAPED THE MODERN MIND writes that 'Laing and his colleagues believed in an entity they labelled the "schizophrenogenic — or schizophrenia-producing — family... Laing argued that investigation of the background of schizophrenics showed that they had several things in common, the chief of which was a family... who behaved in such a way that the person's sense of self became separated from his or her sense of body, that life was a series of 'games' which threatened to engulf the patient'.

Martin's detachable fangs have now been removed, only the empty needle cap in his mouth. The flush of the toilet heralds the imminent arrival of his intended victim, the tension of the waiting moment marked out by evenly spaced piano notes high on the keyboard. Any higher and they might snap and recoil. The flush of the toilet once more draws our attention to the ultimate deromanticising act, the reminder of our common, base physicality. The phantom image of the Hammer siren floating by in her spotless white nightie is dispelled by the reality of bodily functions being attended to. Martin flattens himself against the wall, poised to pounce. We get a glimpse of the red lining of his light jacket coat, a faint echo of the deep red satin flashing out from Dracula's cloak in the Hammer films with Christopher Lee. It is a touch of primary colour in an otherwise bleached-out background.

Paul R. Gagne, in his book THE ZOMBIES THAT ATE PITTS-BURGH, notes that the lighting in **MARTIN** was designed for a black and white film, although it was shot in colour in case this would prove a problem in terms of marketing. On the commentary for the film, Romero and his cameraman talk about shooting on 25 ASA slow reversal stock, positive film that was then reversed to create a negative. It means little to my non-technical brain, but the aesthetic result was a bleached palette which proved perfect for symbolically evoking a world drained of magic, and a town drained of its economic raison d'être, its industrial lifeblood. As ever, Romero and his team adapted to the limited resources at their disposal and turned them to best advantage, like the 'guerilla filmakers' he describes in the documentary on the **MARTIN** special edition DVD.

The door opens and the woman emerges from her pre-bed toilet. Having just taken a piss or a shit, she is now blowing her nose, a further excretion of gross bodily matter which brings disembodied dreaming down to solid earth. There is a close-up of the woman's eyes peering out from the thick, yoghurty layers of a beauty mask, the mechanisms of beauty's construction and maintenance revealed and romantic fancy once more undercut by pronounced and all too human realism. Her cream lathered face has the look of a carnivalesque death visage, as if she has made herself up in anticipation of her imminent fate. It brings to mind the obsession of the Jacobean revenge dramatists with the skull lying beneath layers of beautifying make-up in plague and pox-ridden times.

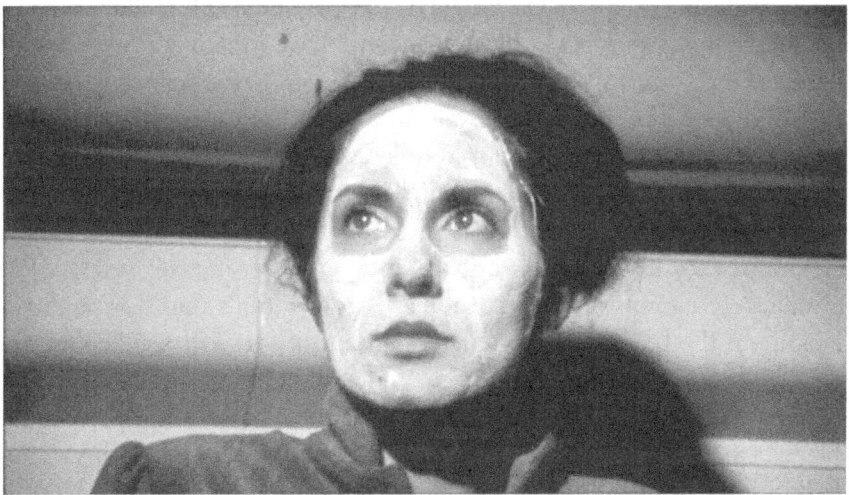

There is a moment of stillness as Martin and the woman look at each other; she stunned by this invasion of her private space, he adjusting to the dramatic contrast of the figure before him from his projected fantasies. Then all is chaos as he launches into his assault and she tries to evade it. Romero's fast editing style ably conveys the impression of violent struggle by cutting between different perspectives, constantly wrenching our angle of vision by filming from above, below and to the side, holding back and then moving in close, maintaining a disorienting sense of the desperate wrestling and tumbling on the bed. As the anaesthetic he has injected into her takes effect and the struggle grows less frantic, Martin pleads with her: "don't scream . . . I just want you to go to sleep". It's a plea that she comply with his fantasies and submit willingly. She doesn't comply and manages to spit out a vehement "freak rapist asshole", once more puncturing his romantic delusions of the ideal woman inviting him in with open, welcoming arms and a smile of delighted anticipation. Her efforts to get him to explain himself—"why won't you say something to me? . . . What do you want?"—are met with silence. A reply, an admission of his hunger, would induce further horror and a renewal of the desperate struggle to escape. Lack of communication and the confusion caused by those who speak a lot but convey little sense is a common theme of Romero's films. He has often said that if the disparate characters holed up together in the ramshackle house in **NIGHT OF THE LIVING DEAD** had only communicated better with one another, they could have united and solved their predicament quite easily. Martin is an almost pathologically taciturn figure. But he does listen attentively and understands people a good deal better for quietly allowing them to fully express themselves. He can also communicate clearly and directly without uttering a word. Silence is often a great deal more eloquent than a relentless stream of empty words.

Martin tries to sooth her, but his attempt at comforting words ("I'm always very careful with the needles…so it doesn't hurt") is woefully lacking in the requisite reassurance. As she drifts into drugged sleep, he caresses her buttock and pulls up the material of her gown. At this point, there is no doubt that he is the freak, rapist asshole of her angry accusation. He is a violent rapist who has used an anaesthetic drug to render his victim helpless and wholly subject to his fantasies. We have no sympathies for him whatsoever. He is a monster.

A cut to a shot of the locomotive light acts as a punctuation point. It is followed up by a close up of a razor blade. The lights have been turned off and Martin is naked. He proceeds to undress her too, with ritualistic care and deliberation. The division of light and shadow above makes a slanting angle across the top of the frame, a nice expressionistic composition. We see the bodies together in outline silhouette. Martin raises up her heavily inert arm and, in agonisingly painful close-up, he draws the razor blade down its length. The lifeblood wells out in viscous, streaming rivulets. There is no question that this is a deathly wound, one from which she will not wake. Martin sups greedily, his mouth and face soon smeared with blood, like a child who has licked and sucked at a melting ice cream cone. The control and clinical efficiency of his preparation is wholly abandoned in the fever of his frenzied feasting. There is a look of almost pathetic desperation as he looks up, his face a blend of self-disgust and satiation.

The long razor slash is a shockingly realistic effect, one which I find difficult to watch (I had to cover my eyes when revisiting the film for this book, as I knew I would). It is also a highly significant moment, in that it marks the entrance of one of Romero's key collaborators, one of the closest members of his extended filmmaking family; in many ways, an adopted 'son', impish and with devil-may-care tendency to push the boundaries of acceptable behaviour, leaving the boss, as he puts it on the **KNIGHTRIDERS** DVD commentary, "pissed at him". But with a good heart, boundless energy and an indefatigable spirit which makes him eager to try his hand at anything. Welcome Tom Savini and his first Romero gore effect.

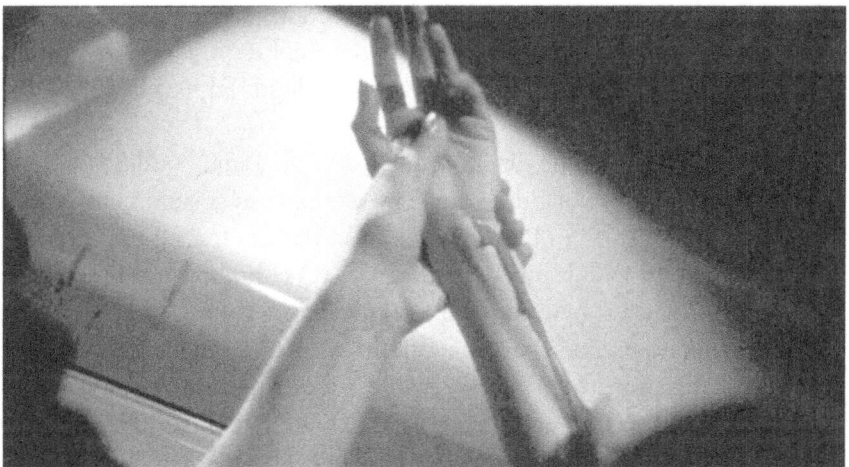

Romero first encountered Savini in 1964, when the latter was still in high school. The director had been looking for young actors for a film project called **WHINE OF THE FAUN**, a picaresque period piece which never got off the ground, and Savini was one of those who auditioned for a major role. His early passion for acting was matched by a fascination with make-up and its transformative possibilities, particularly in the context of horror movies. Lon Chaney was a formative hero. Three years later, whilst studying journalism at Point Park College in Pittsburgh, he heard about the proposed filming of **NIGHT OF THE LIVING DEAD** and called Romero to offer his services as a make-up artist. Alas, before they could meet to discuss the possibility, and before he could show what he was capable of, Savini was called up to serve in the Vietnam war. His

21

experiences there as a combat photographer were highly traumatising, confronting him with the physical reality of violent death. He created necessary distance, and kept his sanity by regarding what he saw in terms of make-up effects. The realism of his visceral gore and make-up effects draw directly upon what he saw, what was captured on the other side of the protective veil of his lens, as he reveals in Adam Simon's 2000 documentary on the new wave of 70s US horror, **THE AMERICAN NIGHTMARE**. Savini met up with Romero again when he auditioned for a role in **MARTIN**, and this time he did get to show off his grisly portfolio. Hired as both actor and make-up effects artist, it was the beginning of a beautiful if blood-spattered friendship. Anecdote has it that he demonstrated his first effect by walking into Romero's office and opening up his own vein, almost causing Christine Forrest to faint. I'd have been on the floor.

We see a close-up of the razor on the floor with a small puddle of blood coagulating along the blade's edge. The woman's eyes stare blankly out, like Marion's dead eye in **PSYCHO** (1960). Martin closes them, shutting off their accusatory lifelessness. The **PSYCHO** comparison is an apt one given the similarities between Martin and Norman Bates. Both are shy, repressed, boyish characters who earn our sympathies to a certain degree in spite of the monstrous acts we witness them perform. After another punctuating cut to the locomotive light, we are back with the compartment light on. The drama has been played out. Martin looks guiltily down on the aftermath of his actions, nervously chewing on his nails. He begins to clear up. It's at this point that the credits start to roll, marking what has come before as a prelude, a shocking revelation of the nature of the titular character. With careful, almost artistic deliberation, Martin lays out the elements of a suicide tableau scene. In the novelisation of the film, written by Susanna Sparrow, who presumably made reference to Romero's script, he throws the body out of the window whilst the train is crossing a bridge over a rocky ravine. This is one of two scenes in the novel which would have made Martin's character a good deal more brutal and hard to sympathise with on any level. They may well have been elements left over from an earlier stage of the production, before John Amplas was cast and put his own stamp on the part. They would have notably coarsened the elegiac tone of the film, and it was wise to leave them out. If indeed they were ever part of a script, or were considered at any point.

A number of razor blades, still in their thick paper wrappers, are left on the floor. A bottle of pills is put on a shelf, then knocked down and scattered to suggest impulsive ingestion. There's a sense that Martin is improvising this tableau as he goes, creating a scenario in his mind. Perhaps even partly erasing his own actions by overlaying them with this theatrical construction. Some of the pills fall across the green eyes of a glamorous black-masked model on the cover of a magazine. She looks like she might be an actress in a modern remake of **LES VAMPIRES** (1915) (something along the lines of Irma Vep, but less self-conscious). This could be another fantasy image from Martin's imagination, but in contemporary colour and looking less liable to invite his advances. This is an image from a women's magazine, representing a world which is alien to him. By the magazine, we see the corner of the BF Skinner book, mind and body side by side. The worlds of advertising and behaviouralist 'operant conditioning' are locked in close orbit. Romero would know about the hidden persuasions and techniques of psychological coercion used by the advertising industry all too well, having done his time in the business. He put his experience to use in **THERE'S ALWAYS VANILLA**, in which a young actress finds work in TV ad spots, obliged to try and infuse a generic beer with sex appeal.

Martin does up the laces of his baseball pumps with an air of purposeful finality. This scene rhymes with one much later in the film, as does the suicide tableau. We will come to them later and find that they provide both a contrast to this calm and coldly unemotional moment and a kind of circular rebalancing of moral indebtedness. This act will have consequences, and the connections will be established through visual parallels. In the bathroom, Martin scrubs away the last of the blood from his face. One last smear on his forehead below his fringe proves difficult to wipe off, however; the 'damned spot' which betokens ineradicable guilt and cursed memory. Back in the compartment, the business of tidying up continues. Martin retrieves his 'fangs', the syringe thrown onto the floor during the struggle. Martin's calmness now that he's had his feed or fix (the empty syringe now suggesting the latter) is marked. Although he uses it to inject his victims rather than himself, the syringe carries associations with addiction, the vampire's hunger as narcotic craving. It's an equation which has been made more or less directly in a number of modern vampire movies, from **ANDY WARHOL'S DRACULA** (1974) (more accurately Paul Morrissey's Dracula aka **BLOOD FOR DRACULA**) through Abel Ferrara's **THE ADDICTION** (1995) and the similarly New York-set **NADJA** (1994), to P.Chih Leong's **THE WISDOM OF CROCODILES** (1998) and Jim Jarmusch's **ONLY LOVERS LEFT ALIVE** (2013). The camp parody of **ANDY WARHOL'S DRACULA** aside, these films are characterised by decaying urban settings. Remove the vampire's class privileges and place them in the modern city and they immediately take on something of the aspect of the junkie.

He clears up in a businesslike way which makes him look as if he really is the cleaner. He even has bin bags amongst his equipment. The cast list comes up during the procedure. Amongst them is the name of the actress whose screen time is effectively already up, aside from a parting corpse shot. Fran Middleton, whom Romero encountered in the New York diner Lady Esthers, along with a number of other cast members. The appearance of her name at this stage feels like a valedictory farewell to her character, as well as an acknowledgement of the importance of her role. Romero has always included strong female characters in his stories, and addressed women's issues in a complex and far from tokenistic manner. Of his 'feminist' film **JACK'S WIFE/SEASON OF THE WITCH** he has said that a lot of the content came from discussions with female friends of his. He is clearly not interested in making a film in which women are objectified victims. As we shall see, the marginalisation of women is one of the factors contributing to the stagnation of the steel town to which Martin is travelling, its inability to reverse its terminal decline.

Martin shuts the door and goes back to his seat, the bag zipped shut. He takes out his paperback book on magic tricks, the manufacture of illusion explained within its pages. Just as the Skinner paperback purported to reveal the mechanisms of human behaviour, so Martin's book exposes the operations of apparent magic. With his dark glasses on, possibly compensating for a sensitivity to light, a diluted version of the vampire's traditional aversion, he relaxes back in his seat. The hunger is in abeyance for a while. It is done.

The guard calls out the Pittsburgh stop, the train pulling into Romero-ville. Romero had moved to Pittsburgh in 1957 when he enrolled in the Carnegie Institute of Technology (Carnegie putting his stamp on institutions of learning again). It became his base of operations for many years afterwards until he upped sticks and moved to Toronto after shooting **LAND OF THE DEAD** (2005) there (**BRUISER** had also been made there in 2000). There's a static landscape shot framed from beneath the canopy of an old, disused part of the station, which looks like an abandoned factory building. The gleaming high-rise bar-graph of the business district is reflected in a puddle, a miniature lake in the rubbled topography of this derelict space. It's a symbolically inverted image, the architecture of finance shooting upwards as money detaches itself from local connections and becomes globally mobile leaving the old industries to decline and die.

In the narrow train corridor, a group of boisterous, animated women, out for a good time on the town by the looks of it, call out for someone called Joyce, hammering on the door of the dead woman's compartment. For a second, we feel like we might have a name to put to the memory of her face, that these might be friends paying a surprise visit on her solitary journey. But the real Joyce appears at the end of the corridor, much to their delight, and we realise that they'd been knocking on the wrong door. Martin has to squeeze past them with his bag held aloft, unable to engage with a group of self-assured women who dominate this space with such cheerful confidence. They call out a smarmy businessman on his sexism, one of them remarking "watch your hands". Together in their female solidarity, they can easily deal with someone like him.

In this exchange, Romero acknowledges the second wave of feminism which had made such an impact on women's lives in the 1970s. It's significant in that it offers a glimpse of vivid life before we move on to a dead town dominated by patriarchal values and marginalised female lives. Is Romero a feminist director? I'm not sure I'd go that far, although he clearly has sympathies with the women's movement. **THERE'S ALWAYS VANILLA** highlighted the sexism actresses routinely encounter in the advertising business and included a disturbing abortion sequence revealing the hidden underside of free love evangelism (a scene every bit as upsetting as the back street abortion scene in Alfie, if not more so). JACK'S WIFE/SEASON OF THE WITCH addressed the subject, unfashionable in a youth-fixated age, of middle aged housewives who have been defined as mothers and wives and who experience a crisis of identity once their children grow up and take their first steps out of the home. And he would continue to write strong female characters into his films. Fran in DAWN OF THE DEAD becomes stronger and more independent as the film progresses, and provides a perspective which is at variance with the boys' machismo, the reflexive manifestation of which proves mortally destructive.

Romero has consistently rejected the way of the gun, the valorisation of the traditional male hero with his default recourse to violent action to solve all problems. It is Fran who offers hope for the future, she who pilots the helicopter which she has learned to fly away from the mall, now hopelessly infested with the living dead. Romero is an artist steeped in bohemian countercultural values who has always valued the ideal of a society in which the whole rich diversity of humanity is allowed free expression and given the opportunity to make a constructive contribution to the health of the whole. He has attempted to fulfil such ideals in microcosm through his own working practices, his determination to remain independent and to foster a creative community rooted in a particular locale. They find full expression in KNIGHTRIDERS, another of his most personal films, and one which he also cites, alongside MARTIN, as a favourite. This neo-Arthurian jousting biker movie features more strong and individual female characters in the form of Christine Forrest's grease monkey and Cynthia Adler's lesbian knight. It also confronts the reality of domestic abuse against women in a heartbreaking way, without offering any easy solutions. It's worth emphasising these aspects of Romero's work to counter the potential criticism that MARTIN is just another horror film in which women are terrorised by a psychotic serial killer. I hope to show that he's aware of such aspects of the horror genre, and tries to counter them as much as he endeavours to refashion the traditional gothic elements of the vampire movie. In his afterword to the novelisation, he notes that to characterise Martin as a vampire "is to forgive him in a way".

The act of demythologisation might illuminate his character, but Romero makes it clear that the attempt to understand does not condone behaviours harmful to others.

A close up of the railway tracks includes a pipe which vents clouds of steam. It's like a smoke machine issuing forth billowing waves of stage fog—the mechanics of theatrical atmosphere once more laid bare. This is the modern, industrial version of swirling gothic mists. The 'fog' curls around a stout elderly figure with a beard neatly trimmed to an angular point, dressed in a spotless white suit, who stands erect on the platform, leaning on an elegant cane. He looks like he would be equally at home in the 19th century environs of a middle-European gothic movie as here on a rundown station in Pittsburgh. His costume is that of someone who believes in his own moral purity; a vampire hunters three piece suit. Martin looks down from the train, his expression weary and wary, but also defiant. He knows he will find no welcome or offer of friendship here. For the first time, we feel a glimmer of sympathy for him. Curt introductions are made, blank statements rather than greetings: "You are Martin Matthias. I am Cuda".

Cuda is played by Lincoln Maazel, the father of Lorin Maazel, the famous symphony orchestra conductor (famous enough that Lincoln was often mistakenly referred to as his better known son). Romero makes this connection on the **MARTIN** DVD commentary. Even in the introduction to his interview for the National Council of Jewish Women's Oral History Collection at the University of Pittsburgh, his interlocutor calls him "Lorin Maazel" before swiftly correcting herself. But Lincoln is a fascinating individual in his own right. Not least because of the dedication he and his wife Marie showed in giving their prodigiously talented son the opportunity to express and develop his gift.

Lincoln Maazel came from a musical family of Russian Jewish immigrants. His father was the first violin in the orchestra of the New York Metropolitan Opera. As such, he worked under the baton of the legendary conductor Arturo Toscanini. His mother was an accomplished singer and his brother a prodigy on the piano. Lincoln himself was a fine singer and also played the piano. Later, he sacrificed a potential performing career in the pre-war years to ensure the fostering of his son's musical education. Young Lorin was placed under the tutelage of the composer and conductor Vladimir Bakaleinikoff, and when he moved to Pittsburgh in 1940 to take charge of the Symphony Orchestra there, the Maazels moved with him (Lorin would later become the director of the Pittsburgh Symphony Orchestra from 1988 to 1996). In post-war Pittsburgh, both Lincoln and Marie Maazel became an established part of the musical scene. Marie formed the Pittsburgh Youth Symphony Orchestra and the Pittsburgh Chamber Music Society. Lincoln was a piano and vocal teacher and also established himself as a popular nightclub singer. In 1959, at the age of 56, he began his acting career after answering an audition ad for the Pittsburgh Playhouse, urged on by his wife. His first role was in Agatha Christie's perennial old warhorse THE MOUSE TRAP. There's a nice cross-generational connection between Maazel and John Amplas, both establishing themselves on the boards of the same theatre. Amplas is fulsome in his praise of Maazel, describing him as "a terrific actor. It was truly a pleasure to work with such a kind and generous man". Maazel first teamed up with Romero for a 1975 short called **THE AMUSEMENT PARK**, made for the Lutheran Services Society and designed to illustrate

28

the tribulations of old age. It's interesting to hear his ordinary speaking voice on the Pittsburgh University Oral History Project tape, recorded in 1994. His cultivated New York intonation makes it clear the extent to which he puts on the old world accent in **MARTIN**. It's a vocal performance which brings the immigrant aspects of the town's character to the fore.

Cuda marches off, firmly planting his cane on the tiles, his brisk stride belying his age. He walks beneath the arch of the station's canopy which we have already seen, heading out towards the Oz-like mirage of the business district's dreaming glass monuments. This is the cityscape of conspicuous prosperity, the exclusive corporate high-rises which would feature as a symbol of social division in Romero's **LAND OF THE DEAD**. It is an environment we will soon leave behind to travel on to its complete antithesis in the social spectrum. Even here, all primary colour has been drained away. This is a monochrome city, sketched in with chiaroscuro gradations of white, grey and black. It might as well have been filmed in the black and white originally planned for the film.

Martin limps along behind Cuda, burdened by his bag and whatever symbolic baggage he also carries with him. The encumbrance of the familial curse, perhaps. Or just the encumbrance of family. A distance significant enough to preclude any communication is maintained between them. Martin might as well be Cuda's bagman, the scurrying servant of an immaculately attired nobleman walking abroad. Looking back at the grand façade of the station we see them emerging from the darkness beneath the arcing curve of the canopy, as if they were setting out from a baroque Carpathian castle. The scene is shot from a low angle so that the station building towers above them. There are many beautifully framed compositions marking the progress of Martin and Cuda's walk through Pittsburgh and subsequently Braddock, often adopting a low-angle perspective. This emphasises the physicality of walking along city streets, giving a real impression of distances covered. There is a notable absence of other human beings. This is a depopulated ghost city, bereft of life or vitality. You half expect one of Romero's living dead to stumble into view around the corner. The eerie sense of desolation, of post-catastrophe abandonment, is similar to that captured by Jon Savage in his series of Uninhabited London photographs taken in January 1977, a visual corollary to his writing on punk in the capital. They were included in a recent Tate Britain exhibition entitled *Ruin Lust*, which linked the fashion for gothic ruins with more modern forms of metropolitan decay and ruination. **MARTIN**'s desolately beautiful city portraits would have fitted in perfectly.

The cinematographer on **MARTIN** was Michael Gornick. This was the first time that Romero had wholly ceded camera duties to other hands, an admission that he couldn't do *everything* on set. Gornick had joined Latent Image in 1972 on a relatively informal basis and was a sound assistant on **THE CRAZIES**. He worked on commercials for Latent and Laurel and grew sufficiently proficient for Romero to hand over the shooting of **MARTIN** to him at a very early stage of the production. He was an ideal choice in that he had a native feel for the environment. He was born in Pittsburgh and, as he reveals in THE ZOMBIES THAT ATE PITTSBURGH, 'I have a lot of strong ties to Braddock...I am from that community, and that's basically where my parents grew up. I've seen that community go through a real transition from its heyday to its current decay, so I had a lot of emotional response to it'. That feeling comes through in his camerawork and in his framing, which brings an at times almost poetic element to the portrayal of the town. Gornick would be the director of photography on all Romero's Laurel features until **DAY OF THE DEAD** in 1985.

As they cross under a viaduct, Martin looks ruefully down into another puddle which has filled a declivity in the rugged, rubbish strewn topography of this infertile urban interzone. Smoking chimneys in the background complete the mood of desolation, the last vestiges of industry adding their artificial clouds to the skyline. The walk through the empty city is sountracked by **MARTIN**'s theme, the long, lonesome descending piano figure. It is joined here by a yearning woodwind melody, which has hints of a mournful Eastern European idiom. And then, raising the melancholy mood to a heightened pitch of unbearable sadness, a soaring female soprano voice rides above it all (the voice of Betty Silberman). It sounds almost like Edda dell Orso adding her magic to an Ennio Morricone score.

Martin and Cuda once more emerge from the shadows, their route taking them through the penumbral edges of the city. It's as if Cuda wants to keep to the shadows, to avoid recognition by any acquaintance they might encounter. Martin, the family shame, must be hustled to the local neighbourhood as quickly as possible. The edge of a railway bridge diagonally bisects the frame. Railways are a persistent presence in the film. They are both a reminder of the transport links which used to connect the industrial centres of Pittsburgh and Braddock to markets across the country and, by extension, the rest of the world and a network of possible escape routes from a place where hopes and opportunities have evaporated. Where once the trains carried the steel which made the world's multiplying automobile population, its increase a sign of expanding prosperity and individualism, they now transport a new mobile generation migrating in search of work elsewhere in the country. The demand for steel for the building of the Pennsylvania railroad track system in the 19th century was one of the major sources of the early prosperity of the Edgar Thompson steel mill in Braddock. Indeed, it was named after J.Edgar Thompson, the president of the Pennsylvania Railroad at the time of its construction.

Beyond the edge of the bridge, a building rises in striking white contrast to the shadows. The occupancy of this shining tower is indicated by the sign at the top reading Advertising Associates. It's a wry nod to Romero's own origins in the Pittsburgh film industry, as well as another signifier of the gulf between reality and manufactured fantasy, dreams fashioned to sell product and the ideology which maintains a constant hunger for it; between the rubbish-strewn shadow world underneath the railway arches and the bright dreams of fulfilment and plenty broadcast from the white heights.

When they arrive at a small outlying station, Cuda takes up his position on the platform, cane planted firmly before him, expression fixed and staring straight forward. Martin remains at a discreet distance, as if by private agreement. He turns to go to the toilet, and only then does Cuda turn to look at his retreating form, frowning and making the sign of the cross. There's a beautifully framed shot taken from the footbridge looking down on the twin tracks which symmetrically divide the screen. Steam hisses from pipes, adding more wreaths of neo-gothic mist. Cuda is a small white figure in the middle distance. Alone in the bleak and empty scene, he looks diminished and less imposing, just an old man waiting stoically for a train.

We now have our second toilet scene in the film. A bum is taking a long, leisurely dump in a cubicle without a door, reading a crumpled old newspaper which he may well subsequently use to wipe his ass with. The misinformation and confusion promulgated by the media is one of Romero's recurrent themes, evident from the very beginning in the broadcasts eagerly absorbed by the inhabitants holed up in the besieged house in **NIGHT OF THE LIVING DEAD**. Far from proving illuminating or helpful, they are more of a distraction from the urgency of dealing with the problem directly facing the characters. The implied redundancy and short-term vision of news reporting here may be another oblique swipe at the media. The bum's alternative method of escapism is stashed by his side in the form of a bottle of booze wrapped in the traditional brown paper bag. Martin takes a piss. This is something you'd never see Christopher Lee do in a Hammer Dracula film. The question of whether vampires pee never arises. It would destroy the mystique of their supernatural aura; which is precisely why we see Martin doing it here. He glances back over his shoulder as the bum lights a cigarette. It's as if he's taken up residence here. This is the absolute base level of society, a public toilet as a home or refuge. Romero pointedly depicts all levels of society in **MARTIN**, the inclusion of the full span of the class spectrum part of a thoroughgoing examination of the character of a local community.

The widening gulf between the rich and the poor would become an increasing concern in his films as the Reaganite free market revolution took hold. **LAND OF THE DEAD** was a parable about such divisions, its loyalties abundantly clear. It also marked the point (subsequent to the first flickerings of sentience in **DAY OF THE DEAD**) when Romero's living dead started to become a revolutionary (or counter-revolutionary) force. This theme has been extended in his recent **EMPIRE OF THE DEAD** series for Marvel Comics, which is complicated by the introduction of a vampire elite. Presented in a far more traditional manner than in **MARTIN**, they represent a hidden cabal of the powerful, holding sway in political, financial and corporate circles. Bloodsuckers in the literal and figurative sense. In **MARTIN**, Romero removes the aristocratic glamour of the vampire and returns it to its peasant roots, albeit ones which have been dug up and relocated half way across the world in an industrialised nation. In **EMPIRE OF THE DEAD**, he restores that elite status but recasts it in a modern mould. The old aristocracy of inherited privilege and social standing in a new exploitative guise.

We cut to a shot of Martin frantically running for the train, Cuda scowling contemptuously from the steps. Our view of Martin is subtly shifting. Not a word has been uttered beyond the curt acknowledgements at their first meeting. But we already understand the dynamic of their relationship, which is encapsulated in Martin's breathless attempts to keep up, the contempt visible in Cuda's every look and gesture. He is viewed as a cursed burden, one reluctantly taken up according to the dictates of familial duty. His every move is analysed for its shortcomings, which will then be highlighted and presented as further evidence of a deficient character. It is the kind of familial relationship which can reduce an individual's self-esteem to a point of near-total eradication. If this is how Martin has been treated for the whole of his life, we can begin to understand his extreme introversion, even something of his hidden pathology. The possibility that Martin's cravings may be the result of persistent and ongoing familial abuse, endured from an early, formative age appears increasingly likely.

There is another shot from the interior of the train, looking out at the platform as Martin climbs aboard. The repetition of certain shots creates a formal structure which offers contrast and comparison. This journey is very different in character from the one which began the film. Martin will use the train regularly, not least to gain distance from the stultifying atmosphere of the family home and its surrounding neighbourhood. For now, though, he is stuck with Cuda's comfortless company. The old man puffs on a large and suitably imposing, masculine cigar, a symbol of potency, wealth and standing. Martin adopts his role as observer, the silent watcher. The train window acts as a screen within the screen. It frames a steel mill, a grey massing of thrusting chimneys and vaulted manufactory halls, an industrial version of the aristocratic vampire's looming castle. It is quiescent now, as much of a ruin as Dracula's crumbling stronghold (which he leaves in the novel to migrate to new territories). It's a cue for the guard to call out for Braddock Station.

A low angle shot from platform level makes the train steps look particularly precipitous. A sign reads 'watch your step' as Cuda descends, followed by Martin. It could be a warning of a more metaphorical nature, as Martin now enters Cuda's territory. He limps behind once more, his cowed and hunched bearing echoing Frankensteinian henchmen in the old Universal movies. As they cross the tracks we see a cluster of church spires in the background, their varied forms indicating the mix of the immigrant population, and their continued connection to the culture and beliefs of the old world. Braddock's ethnic make-up in the early 20th century included as significant number of immigrants from Croatia, Slovenia and Hungary, coming over to work in the mills. The camera remains firmly rooted to the ground, foregrounding the debris and litter scattered all around. The positioning of the camera privileges the earthbound over the spiritual. There is more ground than sky in the shot.

A mutt turns and starts to follow Martin, a stray feeling a natural sense of affinity. It's a happy coincidence, one which arises from Romero's tendency to shoot a lot of material so that he has plenty to use in the edit. "Covering his ass" as he says with characteristically modest self-deprecation on the **MARTIN** DVD commentary track. The inclusion of such intuitively shot footage allows scope for such randomly felicitous moments. This particular moment puts me in mind of Keith Morris' photo of Nick Drake walking down a path towards Hampstead Heath), shoulders hunched in the disconsolation of his deep depression (part of the 'last session' of publicity shots taken in 1971). A dog jumps up beside him, as if to try and make some connection, to break through his isolation. John Amplas has something of a Nick Drake appearance in the film, and Martin's introverted character is also reminiscent of Nick's quietly intense persona.

As Martin walks past a car wrecking yard, the crushed cube of a red car is being picked up in the jaws of a crane and swung towards a pile of similarly compressed blocks of steel. It's a small square of primary colour in bleached and dusty surroundings, a hint of life in the process of being discarded. The camera pulls back to reveal piles of these compressed cubes, building blocks for a ruin soon to be dismantled and shipped away. It's a transparent metaphor for the end of industry. The cars which were made from the steel produced in Braddock's mills are now themselves being broken up. The only visible industry in the town is engaged in the final dismantling of the old industry's by-products, which were also the symbols of local prosperity. Braddock, a central part of the north eastern

35

manufacturing belt of the US would become absorbed into what became known in the 1980s as the 'rust belt'. We witness the shift towards that state of decay and desolation here. Martin's first impression of his new hometown is gained through the steady construction of a towering scrapheap. There is a close-up of his face as he watches its crushing machineries, and it is both curious, anxious and lost. Meanwhile, Cuda is waiting, perennially impatient.

More impressionistic shots build up a picture of the neighbourhood, all viewed through Martin's eyes. A pair of sneakers dangles on a wire and battered cars line the sidewalk. We also gain a sound picture of the surroundings, the barking of dogs in the street and the pounding of the breaking yard blending together. This is a poor area. The old white, wooden-boarded and steeply gabled colonial house which Cuda and Martin approach (the Buba family home, in fact) is an anomaly, a spectre of faded gentility. It is entirely in fitting with the old man, its white façade echoing his white suit. Together, they give him the air of an old plantation owner. Martin watches Cuda enter through the garden gate with a downturned mouth, a heartbreaking look. Cuda hasn't waited for him, has offered no invitation to cross the threshold. This is not a home in which he will receive any welcome. He notices a shrine in the garden, an indication of Cuda's staunch Catholicism, conspicuously displayed for all to see. There is a small musical interlude featuring violin, the old country instrument. The wordless female vocal ends on a long held note. This is the place where the journey ends.

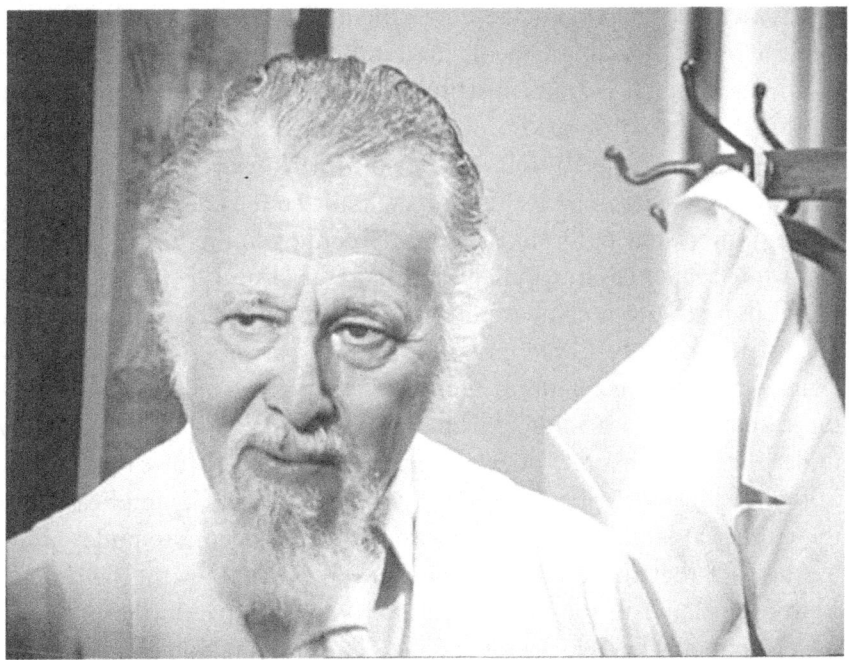

"Nosferatu", hisses Cuda as Martin enters the hall, an anti-greeting which says 'I know what you are'. It's an old world term, apparently originating in the Transylvanian district. Emily Gerard, in her 1885 travel book THE LAND BEYOND THE FOREST, observes 'more decidedly evil, however, is the vampire, or nosferatu, in which every Roumanian peasant believes as firmly as he does in heaven or hell'. The origins of the word are obscure. It may be an amalgam of necurataul, the Romanian word for the devil; nesuferit , Romanian for 'unbearable'; nesophorus, Greek for plague carrier; and nesufuratu, old Slavic for carrier of disease. Nosferatu were traditionally thought to be carriers of plague. Their origins were vague, but

37

one vector of progeniture might be illegitimate birth from illegitimate parents. Nosferatu tended to prey on members of the family, bringing the blight of infertility and barrenness. They were specifically able to have sex with the living, generally whilst they were asleep. Cuda's use of the term implies all of these familial curses. Bram Stoker picked up on the name through his reading of Gerard's book, and he used it a handful of times in DRACULA. F.W. Murnau drew from Stoker when looking for a title for his 1922 cinematic adaption of the novel, the novelist's widow having denied him the use of the name Dracula (and indeed the right to adapt the book in any fashion). It is from this film, a classic of German expressionist horror, that the word has become widely familiar. This word, with its embodiment of forgotten folk beliefs and myths revived and given new form by the movies, is perfect for the thematic context of **MARTIN**.

We immediately cut from the curse of naming to the first of the black and white sequences in which a short-haired Martin is confronted by an exorcism party, presumably featuring members of his old family. They are dream memories or filmic fantasies, a theatrical superimposition over-laying what may be genuinely traumatic experiences. The way in which these sequences are intercut with the unfolding narrative repeatedly underlines the proximity of direct experience with subconscious fantasy influenced by cinematic images in Martin's mind, and by implication in the culture at large. The dreamlike ambience is once more undermined by the fact that the exorcism sequence takes place in the bathroom, Martin cornered in the most private of domestic spaces (the only one which generally has a lock on the door). The combination of fast cutting, broad gestural action within the static frame and tilted angles give these sequences a real dramatic, kinetic quality. They are anti-naturalistic, recre-ating an older, expressionistic cinematic language. As such, they provide a contrast with the naturalistic tone of the rest of the film in terms of form and style as well as in the shift from colour to black and white. This anti-naturalism, the strongly pronounced cinematic qualities of these sequences, strongly suggests that these are not Martin's memories but rather dreams and fancies.

Some critics have found fault in the film for Romero's supposed failure to state whether Martin is or is not an actual vampire. Tom Milne, in his

Sight and Sound review, writes that 'much of the charge...is unfortunately undermined by the film's failure to confront (let alone resolve) the paradox presented by its rationalisation of the vampire myths. Having his cake and eating it, as it were, Romero characterises his hero simultaneously as a troubled teenager and as an age-old vampire kept youthful by infusions of blood'. Richard Combs, in his *Monthly Film Bulletin* review, includes the black and white sequences amongst his list of the film's 'stray distractions', 'supposedly depicting how Martin has always been hounded by his fellow men, but confusingly suggesting at times that they might just be Martin's present-day fantasies, or his disordered recollection of those misleading movies'. Presumably such ambiguity and structural experiment would have been considered perfectly acceptable were this a European art movie.

Richard Lippe, in his essay 'The Horror of Martin' in the critical collection on 70s US horror THE AMERICAN NIGHTMARE, which he and Robin Wood edited at the end of the decade, is less judgemental, but suggests that 'the premise on which the film is based, an age-old vampire living in a modern world, is subtly evaded by Romero's seemingly open-ended narrative. Romero has devised an elaborate film structure so that the film can be read as saying Martin is a vampire or that he is, like everybody else, a victim of a barren society'. But the clues are there, embedded in the formal structure of the film and in its abiding thematic concerns. Lippe goes on to acknowledge this: 'In reality, the film endorses the second interpretation by being centred on the concept of fantasy'. Romero has never been one to impose his own interpretations on his own films. He has remarked that he finds critical appraisals which uncover 'hidden' or unconscious meaning within his work frustrating because it's all there on the surface, *deliberately* presented. His comments on **MARTIN**, including his cogent afterword to the novelisation, have always made it plain that he doesn't think of his character as an actual vampire. In the short documentary included with the expanded DVD edition, he says "I don't think he's a vampire. I just think he's messed up".

To me, this has never been in question. The film questions society's need for monsters, for monstrous scapegoats, and demonstrates its tendency to create and renew them, refashioning them to fit in with the

times. Through familial predestination and constant reinforcing suggestion, Martin has internalised these needs and amalgamated them with his
own repressed desires. He gives his family and the wider society exactly the
monster they require, cast in an archetypal form which is universally
recognised.

"First I will save your soul, then I will destroy you", Cuda bluntly tells
Martin, still waiting before him in the hallway. It's not much of a
welcome. The house rules are laid down with terrible finality. Cuda also
reveals the primitive and merciless form of religion to which he adheres,
full of Old Testament violence and absolutism. Martin may receive salvation on a spiritual level, but his body will still bear the stain of the family
curse, an ineradicable genetic inheritance. Salvation is the prelude to
death. They ascend through more narrow, constricting white corridors,
crucifixes fixed to the walls with one more nail. Martin is shot looking
disconsolately through the bannisters, barred in to these restrictive
passageways, the home already feeling like a prison.

Garlic hangs from closed bedroom doors. As they ascend one final set of
stairs to Martin's attic room, the space between the walls narrower than
ever, we hear a steady drum thump once more; the anticipatory heartbeat
heralding some terrible revelation or burst of violent action. Here, it

sounds like the slow funereal thud of a military drum marking out the final processional steps to the scaffold. The mournful female voice sings a folkish lament with echoes of the Dies Irae.

Martin's attic room is a claustrophobic white space devoid of any homely detail. Cuda in his white suit almost blends into its blank walls, the lines of contrast becoming indistinct without any colour variation. There seems no place to hide in its glaring confines. Cuda whips away the cloth covering a mirror with a wicked, vulpine smile. But Martin's reflection is thrown back at him from its polished glass. It is the first refutation of his beliefs. But nothing can dispel them, no evidence turn him from his conviction that Martin is a monster. It is a breed of monster which he has need of to maintain his worldview, a moral and spiritual disorder over which he can exert control by following the old ways. Martin's failure to obey the dictates of vampire lore by casting no reflection in the mirror merely angers him. It's as if Martin were being deliberately obtuse by refusing to display his authentic traits.

"Pamgri", Cuda spits out with hateful vehemence, a branding of Martin as monster which parallels his earlier victim's "freak rapist asshole". "Pamgri" is an interesting word to use here, one which would no doubt be unfamiliar to most viewers. It is an old and obscure Hungarian word for vampire, dating from the time when the district of Transylvania was still part of Hungary and, by extension, of the Austro-Hungarian empire. It is quoted in an 1810 volume with the exhaustive if rather blandly literal title TRAVELS OF THREE ENGLISH GENTLEMEN FROM VENICE TO HAMBURG, DOING THE GRAND TOUR OF GERMANY IN THE YEAR 1734, which in turn cites the 1733 tome DISSERTATIO DE VAMPIRIS SERVIENSIBUS by one John Heinrich Zopfius, viz. 'the Hungarians call these spectres pamgri'. This use of unfamiliar words blended with more everyday language gives an authentic feel of first generation immigrant speech, with its distinctive variations in phrasing and idiom.

Cuda's cry of "pamgri" is intercut with two flashes of the black and white Martin turning from the bathroom mirror, alerted by the first words of the rite of exorcism. Real and dream selves are mirrored in a bedazzling, illusory juxtaposition. It's like one of the old illusionistic games (the sort which fascinate Martin) where a card disc bears a picture of a bird on one side, a cage on the other. By winding attached strings up and letting the disc spin freely around, the bird appears to be in the cage. The black and white Martin, an inhabitant of daydream and fantasy, has been created by Cuda and his familial kind with their rigid, unassailable beliefs and wild, vindictive (and self-vindicating) accusations. Romero establishes direct points of connection between the real and fantasy sequences throughout, whether in terms of objects or actions. In this case, it is the mirror which links the two, as well as the incantatory words of damnation. I'm making the assumption from this point onward that the black and white sequences are products of Martin's imagination rather than actual memories. These links which Romero carefully includes would seem to suggest that this is the case, and it would certainly fit in with the general theme of disillusionment, of facing up to reality, no matter how bleak and comfortless.

Cuda lays down the law with the emphatically stabbing finger of the righteous and aggressively self-important. "You may come and go, but you will not take people from the city". It's a very nimbyish sentiment and which betokens a moral outlook narrowly defined by neighbourhood boundaries. This is the kind of perspective which turns a blind eye on what happens beyond the limits of familiar territories. Effectively, it solves a problem by relocating it elsewhere, giving the vampire license as long as he sates his hunger in foreign territories. Blood is thicker than water, it would seem, and familial standing in the local community more important than the lives of unknown victims. It could also, at a stretch, be seen as a metaphor for Cold War realpolitik. Atrocity and human rights abuses are accepted in foreign, state-sponsored dictatorships, all in the name of holding back the expansion of the Eastern bloc and keeping markets open for the safe conduct of American corporate business.

"I have been told you are imbecile", Cuda states. Told by whom? Where has Martin come from? From which household has he been expelled and for what reason? His origins remain something of a mystery, a story left untold. "Speak, Nosferatu!" Cuda commands. A low angle shot peers upward so that Martin appears hemmed in by the slanting, narrowing lines of the attic room roof, trapped in its restrictive pen. Cuda leaves the room, assured that Martin is indeed a creature worthy of his contempt. This cues up the black and white bathroom exorcism fantasy once more. In this instance, Martin grabs the crossed candles aggressively held out in front of him to bar his exit. The camera zooms back from its oppressive close-up. It's a technique which Romero rarely uses, which makes its employment here all the more startling. It opens up the space with a suddenness which suggests a psychological breakthrough. Martin's dream self pushes the candles aside and breaks through in a physical sense. This precipitates his actions in the real world. These black and white sequences often feel like rehearsals for decisive acts, as if Martin has to play out the fantasy scenario in his mind before the actual one can be performed.

He tumbles down the stairs ('watch your step!') in a mad rush. Cuda swiftly locks himself in his bedroom (bedrooms as well as bathrooms have locks in this house of secrecy and paranoia). The voices droning the Latin liturgy from the dream exorcism are echoed and stretched out into a white noise hiss, sounding as if they were coming from far away in time and space. This stretching also acts as an expression of Martin's emotional state, the white noise hiss of rage as he is pushed past the breaking point. The demonization of the dream exorcists is linked with Cuda and his hateful imprecations. Martin comes out with his first refutation of magic, his call to recognise the real. It's a point he will repeatedly try to make, using a variety of devices to get his message across. Again, the statement is rehearsed in the dreamworld first: "There isn't any magic, it's just a sickness". Having made this assertion in the dream theatre, he breaks into the bedroom, the garlands of garlic hung from the door unsurprisingly proving useless as a repellent. Cuda has grabbed his small ivory rosary crucifix out of a dressing table drawer. The mirrors at the back hint at a wife now gone. Perhaps the small, delicate rosary was hers too. A plaster figurine of Mary rocks on the table surface. This is a bedroom with a surprisingly female ambience. As it threatens to teeter over and smash, the basis of Cuda's faith also seems to be in the balance. He needs this obsession with casting Martin as an unholy creature, an incarnation of satanic evil in the world. It shores up the foundations of his belief, gives it a focus when all around him has become unstable and beyond his control. Martin is his sacred monster.

There is a close up of Cuda thrusting the cross out before him in the traditional (or received) Van Helsing manner; the vampire hunter in white with his white crucifix. We then cut to a wider shot, with Martin sprawled on the bed onto which he had just dived and Cuda crouching, small and fearful, at its foot, the pocket cross seeming tiny and barely noticeable in his palsied hand. It's a far cry from the large and sturdy wooden affairs wielded by Peter Cushing and his cinematic Van Helsing brethren. As Martin rises up, Cuda hisses "Nosferatu" once more. In his eyes, the nature of the beast has finally been revealed. The last dying sussuration of the dream litany fades away, leaving a tense silence. "Nosferatu" doesn't attack, however. Instead, he speaks, as previously commanded. But it is not the kind of confessional which Cuda expected and desired. Martin gives an impassioned, angry and, finally, agonised refutation of Cuda's superstitious aggregation of vampire lore. But first he introduces himself properly, emphasising his relation to the old man. "I am your cousin—your cousin Martin". It is a simple statement of identity and familial connection which cuts through all the occult mystification of Cuda's pronouncements. Indeed, it's an almost comical moment. The terrifying Nosferatu, the ancient Pamgri reveals his true name—and it is utterly, disarmingly ordinary. It is the starting point for a further programme of demystification. Martin's repeated refrain, which he returns to at various points in the film, is "you see", a direct appeal to the empirical evidence of the senses. It's uttered here as he rips down a chain of garlic and chomps on one of the bulbs (a fine display of stoicism by John Amplas here, who manages to refrain from grimacing, choking or spluttering out the raw and pungent stuff) and snatches the crucifix from Cuda's hand. "It isn't magic", he adds as he wipes the crucifix he has snatched from Cuda's hand across his sweaty brow, 'infecting' it with his essence, his sickness—the plague which the Nosferatu carry with them. His burst of anger quickly spent, he attempts to reason with Cuda. "Even I know that", he says with telling self-effacement. His voice is now quiet and gentle, as if he pities the old man with his absurd delusions; even if those delusions threaten his own well-being. He retreats and shuts the door which he has just violently forced open carefully behind him, allowing Cuda his privacy once more. It is he who is now speechless.

We cut from this depiction of the old man cowed to a confident Cuda in the community. He talks with a black man as he walks along the street. It is a very diverse neighbourhood, and it remains so in the present day. A significant component of the remaining post-industrial population of Braddock is African-American (66.52% according to a 2000 census). A gaggle of brightly-clad middle-aged ladies wait outside Cuda's grocery store. He is evidently late opening up, perhaps still rattled by yesterday's incident. "You need help here", one of the ladies tells him, not without sympathy. He is clearly well known to them, a respected and well-regarded local figure who invites a certain kind of formal familiarity. He explains that "my cousin has come in from Indianapolis". A further layer of mundane history is thus added to Martin's character, a further element of mystery removed. There is nothing of the passing on of the family curse here, rather the implication that Martin has travelled to Braddock especially to help him out in the shop. He explains that he "is a young man—not even 20", placing Martin as a 19 year old, on the verge of leaving his teens. Beyond the home, talk of Nosferatu and evil inheritance is abandoned, appearances scrupulously kept up. Indeed, Cuda even defends Martin against the vituperative moral inquisition of one of the ladies, Mrs Bellini, who questions his presence in the same house as Cuda's granddaughter Christina (who is mentioned for the first time here). "It looks how you want it to look", he says, adding "my family knows how to behave". A double-edged statement if ever there was one.

A cut to a close up of an eye on the cover of Martin's paperback book on magic tricks creates an ironic counterpoint to Cuda's assertion that his family is the acme of respectability, and that appearances are in the subjective eye of the beholder. Martin is far from being a normal young man, and the pseudo-occultism of the cover reminds us of Cuda's previously stated beliefs. It also takes us back to the scene preceding Cuda's assertion of normality and propriety, to Martin's declaration that "there is no magic". This is a book which teaches the art of deception, of illusionism. "It looks how you want it to look". Martin has his tinted glasses on as he reads the book. It's another piece of demythologisation; the vampire's aversion to daylight merely a mild sensitivity to light. Martin plays with a small guillotine, one of the magical toys which he has brought with him which

45

show his fascination with the mechanics of the impossible, that which seemingly defies natural law; theK supernatural, in effect. He puts his finger through the hole beneath the blade and pulls the lever which brings it sharply down. No blood is shed. 'Comical' pizzicato string music with jaunty piano accompaniment is suggestive of a light interlude, a scherzo. But the close up of a stick of celery being sliced along its length by a keen blade has uncomfortable echoes of a razor being drawn down a raised arm. Just as this parallel is been drawn, Martin has his first awkward meeting with Christina, who enters at this point. Startled from his absorption in his enigmatic endeavour, he runs out to a bench in the garden. Local kids are playing in the back streets, and a biker idles over. His "hey, what's happening?" is an invitation to join in, to become a part of his generation. But Martin just turns around. The backyard is a no-man's-land between family and home and the community beyond.

Christina is played by Christine Forrest, later to become Christine Romero. Romero wrote the role for her, as he had done for John Amplas. Having graduated from college in Florida in 1969, she had been a struggling actress in New York for a number of years in small theatrical productions. Her parents lived in Pittsburgh and it was during one of her visits that she met Romero. An audition for **MARTIN** ensued, and she was immediately given the part. She had roles in all of Romero's subsequent films up until **BRUISER** in 2000, notably her portrayal of the tomboy mechanic Angie in **KNIGHTRIDERS**. She has also worked as a producer, assistant director and casting director. Her performance in **MARTIN** has a naturalistic air perfect for the tenor of the film.

Back inside, Christine is cooking in the kitchen and Martin returns, leaning silently back against the wall. The kitchen becomes the room in the house where Martin feels most comfortable, a 'female zone' partly sheltered from Cuda's patriarchal control. Although his presence is absent, his rule still abides. Christina is cooking stuffed cabbage, a popular Hungarian and Romanian dish, which is "Tata" Cuda's favourite; and "round here things are done his way".

Tata is a Romanian familiar name for father, its use, along with the preparation of a dish from the old country, another indication of origins and the persistence of immigrant culture in a new land. Martin doesn't respond to Christina's conversational gambits, but seems fascinated by the radio, which is burbling out a local talk show. It appears to be acting as an on-air confessional. He hunkers down to listen to it, seemingly preferring this remote communion to the possibility of direct communication with somebody immediately present. Communication, or the lack of it, is the focus of this scene. Christina talks of having a phone extension installed in her room, a preparation for a retreat into a private domestic space, a personal cell enclosed within a house dominated by the spirit of the pater familias. She reaches out to Martin, asking him whether he'd like a phone too. It's an ironic way of trying to connect with him, by offering him the possibility of remote communication, of actually increasing the distance. The only hope she can envisage is in reaching beyond the limiting environment of home and locality, of creating some sort of connection with the wider world beyond.

A family meal has the awful, edgily funny feel of a Mike Leigh scene. Awkward silence prevails until Cuda observes "look how he eats", as if he were a curious and grotesque specimen. Martin's every move seems to be under scrutiny, and Christina looks suitably embarrassed for him. Martin chooses this moment to bring out his toy guillotine. Having beheaded his sliced celery with a decisive downward thrust of the blade, he invites Christina to put her finger in a second hole, above the first. It's the first time we've heard him speak to her. She declines, laughing, and so he puts his own finger in place. He pauses for effect, building up tension with a natural sense of theatrical timing before bringing the blade down. The celery is severed with a wet crunch, but his finger remains intact. Christina laughs with a blend of startlement and delight (an authentic Christine Forrest laugh according to Romero and his fellow DVD commentators) and Martin smiles at her response. It's the first time we've seen him smile, the first time he's really made a connection with someone. His fascination with magic and its mechanics brings him out of himself and allows him to express himself more freely. It's a nice metaphor for the way performance and art can provide introverted personalities with the means to articulate their feelings, views and experiences—their hidden selves.

Cuda, of course, reacts to the trick with a disapproving glower. Martin's demonstration brings a much needed element of warmth to the table, breaking the tense atmosphere with laughter and surprise, with light-hearted play that undermines Cuda's dour, puritanical outlook. He has an underlying message to impart as well, however, one which he attempts to deliver time and again in various guises. He explains the mechanics of the toy, the slip blade which can be withdrawn; and then he looks directly at Cuda, a serious expression transforming his face. "There's no magic ever", he concludes, his realist's credo. Cuda has pledged himself to saving Martin's soul. In a way, Martin is attempting to bring enlightenment into Cuda's life, to destroy the illusions which so narrowly define his world. It's an intergenerational struggle between an old, proscriptive morality and a new, open and questioning way of life, freed of the inheritance of delimiting values. Martin could be Cuda's saviour, his illuminating angel.

Martin's refutation of magic, the conclusion of his trick, is the cue for the entrance of Arthur, Christina's boyfriend. It's entirely appropriate since Arthur is played by Tom Savini, the special effects maestro; Martin's celery slicing succeeded by the appearance of the man who created the vein slashing effect. The message of disenchantment is also followed by the introduction of a character who represents the disillusionment of the generation thrown on the scrapheap, unable to find the meaningful work which their parents had taken for granted. Adding a further level of deromanticism, it soon becomes apparent that whatever magic may once have ignited Arthur and Christina's relationship has been dispelled by a combination of social hardship, familial pressure and simple ennui.

Arthur is warmly greeted by Cuda, however, the most animated we have yet seen him. They are the men of the house, sharing masculine values. Cuda peremptorily introduces Martin as his cousin from Indianopolis, the default line for outsiders (Arthur not yet privy to the family secrets). The masculine talk immediately falls to the employment situation. "I hear there's work there", Arthur says, half questioning. It's not a line which Martin is likely to respond to, lost as he is in his own self-absorbed world. Realist he may be, but it's not the kind of realism which encompasses views on politics or the state of the economy. Cuda is ready with his reflexive, Norman Tebbit-like response, however, an expression of firmly entrenched views which require no evidence to back them up. "There's work everywhere", he states. "People just don't bother to look for it". The blame is thus placed firmly on the individual, social circumstances ignored. It's the same worldview which attributes Martin's 'sickness' to a family curse, ignoring the effect a corrosive family environment might have had on his development. Throughout the film, family and wider society are inextricably linked, the former a microcosm of the latter. Conservative political ideologies often place great value in 'family values' alongside an insistence on economic individualism. Cuda's stubborn adherence to old superstitions in the face of all contrary evidence and his insistence that economic problems are rooted in individual indolence rather than some wider systemic collapse or fundamental economic shift are two forms of inflexible conservatism. Both opt for the comforting illusion of continuity with a past which is itself partly a nostalgic fantasy of 'simpler' times. He is, in effect, a proto-Reaganite.

Martin runs upstairs, driven out by this male usurpation of a feminine space he had begun to feel comfortable in. His connection with Christina is a significant one. They are both, in their own way, marginalised within the house, as the following scene makes clear. There are four cuts jumping from a mid to near to close to extreme close focus on the polished, blank china face of an old doll in the corner of Martin's room. Its fixed expression seems to mock the sacrosanct ideal of family values as we overhear Arthur and Christina arguing loudly in the bedroom downstairs. It is the child they will never have. And what is it doing here? Was Martin's room originally intended as a nursery? Are these the toys which Christina's mother might have played with? Perhaps they even belonged to Cuda himself. They certainly have a look of Victorian antiquity to them. Other dolls have impassive, eavesdropping faces, unemotional and non-responsive to the domestic ructions unfolding downstairs.

Martin sits by the window playing with an old wooden toy, a brightly painted peasant figure which is made to jump over a fence by the thumbing of a trigger. Martin puts it through its repetitive motions, a toy once more expressing something of the secretive thoughts passing through his mind. There's a brittle frustration to his reflexive triggering of the peasant's jerking leaps, a barely suppressed anger at what he cannot help but hear. Christina is complaining that Arthur is spending too much time with Cuda "watching the game", a masculine bond which has excluded her, driving her to the refuge of her bedroom. Arthur is under Cuda's spell, co-opted into the paternalistic values of the household and inducted into its hierarchies. Romero's sensitivity to the women's movement comes to the fore once more here and elsewhere in **MARTIN**. Christina is evidently supposed to know her place within the house (and the house is her place), and that place is the kitchen. It's the only place we generally encounter her. "Gimme a break", Arthur says as we tune out of the argument.

Martin begins to drift off on the sill by the open window whose curtains are drifting in a gentle breeze on this somnolent afternoon. It's our first view of Martin as cat. Romero has commented on John Amplas' grace, the dancelike qualities of his performance. On the DVD commentary to **MARTIN** he refers to his "moves" as being "almost classical", and notes in particular the way he ducks his head before standing up, almost as if he's falling before rising. It's his equivalent of the Kinski rise and turn into the camera which Werner Herzog always found so mesmerising. It's something which really comes out in his role as the mime in **KNIGHTRIDERS** and, in a different way, in his rolling zombie walk in **CREEPSHOW**, each step seeming the prelude to a collapse which never quite happens. Martin will later be likened to a cat, but there are several scenes in the meantime in which his feline qualities are quite apparent.

He is woken from his reverie by the rude knocking of a hammer. Cuda is knocking in nails from which to hang a string of tiny bells which will tinkle whenever Martin opens the door. When Martin opens the door and realises what has been done, Cuda looks up at him with a face like an evil moon, eyes narrowed and teeth bared in a triumphant grin. It's at times like these when we realise how much he needs Martin. These moments when he asserts his dominance are the only occasions when he evinces real pleasure, when he smiles in his malevolent fashion. This scene is directly connected to the one preceding it. Cuda has consolidated his paternalistic authority over both Martin and, through Arthur, Christina. He is making it known that he is the unquestioned master of the house, and will know of all the comings and goings of its inhabitants. Martin responds with one of his desolate looks, mouth downturned, looking out

from the threshold of his room which he will not now be able to cross without sounding this primitive alert—the alarm bells. The mournful female vocals express his sorrowful soul. The fact that Martin's musical leitmotifs are feminine suggests that he is more comfortable in the female world. He has no place in the male hierarchies. It's perhaps another reason why he has been rejected by his family. Is there a hidden gay subtext to Martin? It's possible, although it's not one I will explore here. In a way, vampires possess a sexuality all of their own. In his book VAMPYRES:LORD BYRON TO COUNT DRACULA, Christopher Frayling coins the term 'haemosexuality', which he considers 'the most apt general term to describe the sexual basis of the vampire relationship'.

A **KES**-like flute over impressionistic Bill Evans piano chording accompanies Martin as he we see him out of the home and wandering around town in a carefree fashion, making deliveries for Cuda. The flute here is played by Steve Gorn, a jazz musician who has also displayed a sustained interest in Indian music. He has played the Indian bamboo flute on a number of recordings, some released on the highly-respected European ECM label, and has recorded in the distinguished company of the likes of Jack de Johnette, Badal Roy, Nana Vasconcelos and Tony Levin. There's a beautifully framed shot creating a symmetrical composition with the arches covering a railway bridge. Their vanishing perspective leads the eye to the autumnal trees on the hills opposite. There really are some beautiful shots in **MARTIN**, Mike Gornick's familiarity with the terrain no doubt coming into play. This one captures the seasonal mood perfectly. There's something of Jack Kerouac's elegiac evocations of small town memories in novels such as DOCTOR SAX and VISIONS OF DULUOZ to these scenes—hints of Ray Bradbury too. These are the leafy suburbs, hence the pastoral flute. The omnipresence of the railways, the old economic conduits of the town which now offer an escape route, is once more evident here too.

An old lady in a tree-shaded wooden house gives Martin a tip and pats him on the head as if he were a friendly dog. His taciturnity is taken for simple-mindedness. But he is popular with women, they respond to his quiet docility. And he in turn seems more comfortable in female company. He next visits the house of Mrs Santini, a middle-aged woman with a dreamy air about her whom we see in medium close up as she comes to the door. As with the previous delivery, he waits on the threshold. It will be some time before he responds to the invitation to cross it. Martin looks non-plussed by Mrs Santini. We follow his gaze and see her in full-length profile back in the hall. She doesn't have a skirt on, and casually picks one up to wrap around her bare legs. She notices him looking, and then quickly averting his eyes. She offers him a lift. We have a shot from the inside of the house as she puts the food away in the fridge. There is Martin, still waiting on the threshold, beyond the mesh door cover. Mrs Santini is played with a nice air of gin-blurred weltanschauung by Elyane Nadeau, whom Romero met through a film business acquaintance of Richard Rubinstein. MARTIN appears to have been her only film appearance (she passed away in 2005) which is a shame.

The car drives off, heading steeply down from the houses on the hill as Mrs Santini 'delivers' Martin back downtown. The music is now a light blend of piano and violin, with a hint of Jean-Luc Ponty. There is a subtle shift in tone. Martin is no longer wandering alone, lost in his own world, but is in the car with someone else, someone outside the family. The violin, introduced here for the first time, has a more worldly sound than the airy, pastoral flute. This is effectively Mrs Santini's theme. It also befits the drive into a more built up, commercial district of the town.

A view from the interior of the car offers a visually punning screenwipe as soapy suds are squeegeed away by an automated washer. This suddenly seems like a very intimate space, the world outside kept at a distance. Mrs Santini makes bitter reference to her husband, "off gallivanting with the girls". This is maybe why she wanted to have Martin here, as a captive yet neutral audience. She refuses to use money for the gas since "I don't get enough as it is". This is marriage as an economic partnership, love long left lying. The suburbs, with their elevated prospect and spacious and modern detached houses, may look more prosperous than the downtown areas of Braddock. But the professionals and businessmen who live there still have to travel some distance to work. And once more, women are marginalised, excluded from the workforce and left lovelessly at home.

Martin looks agitated at the way the front seats of the car are turning into a confessional. Mrs Santini asks him to reach into the glove compartment for a little black notebook in which she keeps her accounts. Again, a deromanticising detail - marriage reduced to accountancy, figures in columns balancing the rote financial framework of an emotional void.

The glove compartment has a jumble of small, everyday objects amongst which are Tampax. Martin is in a female space, but this is not so comfortable for him. The feminine mysteries are rather too prominently displayed here. "If you don't like it, get out", Mrs Santini says, engaging in a dialogue with herself. Martin takes the opportunity to exit, however, whether he misunderstands or not. His self-esteem is so low that he is almost expecting such an offhand dismissal. But Mrs Santini is quick to disabuse him of this misunderstanding. She wants him there and is not prepared to let him escape. And now comes the direct feline comparison. She says "you remind me of an old cat I used to have", one which she could talk to as it wouldn't talk back, wouldn't judge her. John Amplas acts in a very expressive way with his eyes in this scene, a performance style harking back to the era of silent movies. Whether as a monster or as a cat-like listener, Martin acts as a repository for people's unexpressed emotions.

Mrs Santini drops Martin off by the Cuda Co. sign, and he stands beneath it, his back to the family. A last minute gesture, a raised arm and a 'thank you' is all she needs. Contact has been made. And Martin has taken his first steps into the world beyond the family home. Cuda watches with a suspicious eye from the shop door window. Martin is showing the first signs of independence, of slipping beyond his control. We cut from this scene of paternalistic scrutiny to the sound of a slowly creaking door and the light jingle of bells, blending in with the stridulating night chorus of crickets outside. Martin lurks by his door, held marginally ajar so that the bells don't betray his presence. It's another shot of him on the threshold, watching from the wings. The faint sound of the bells and the low-level ambient sounds of the natural world create an aura of magical suspension, a sense that the fixed boundaries of time and place have lost their definition, given way to a vague, indeterminate drift. Down in the living room, Christina and Cuda are looking through a book of old, sepia-tinted photographs. It is actually the Buba family album, the ancestors of Grandma Buba and, even more distantly, of Pat and Tony. It reminds of how close Buba is to Cuda. Just a couple of neighbouring consonants in the alphabet separates them. Romero's naming of his imposing patriarch was a little homage, perhaps, a thankyou for grandma Buba's graceful hosting of his film-making family.

Cuda, holding the book of memories which he is the last living soul to have direct possession of, uses it as a prop to outline the family inheritance; a genetic and cultural inheritance but also a bond of absolutist faith, inviolable and wholly immune to reason. "Your mother knew, she believed", Cuda tells Christina. It's a reference to an absent female presence in the house, a mother whom Christina was too young to know. In this calmly elucidated mythology of family, Cuda reveals that "Martin had his father until he was 32". There is no mention of a mother at this stage. It's as if she is of secondary importance, the female influence scarcely worthy of mention. "He is Nosferatu", he adds as an evenly stated matter of irrefutable fact, born in 1892 with parentage in the old country. This is the savant moment, the part in the story where the vampire hunter, armed with his woodcut-illustrated antiquarian volumes, explains the nature of the beast. The past doesn't go away in a society populated by successive waves of immigrants. Stories of origins are passed down from generation to generation, history and fiction blended until the dividing lines are hopelessly erased.

The flipping of the family album is beautifully shot in close-up with a soft focus clarity and sepia haze lending it the air of a dream parade of half-glimpsed ghosts. There is a close-up of the family photo on the sidetable, the camera making another surprise zoom back to incorporate Cuda in his armchair, the photo now a small framed presence in the background. The link between past and present is made explicit. This is a house which is haunted by the past, by unspoken spectres. Except that they are spoken now, in this scene in which Cuda, in his own way, attempts to communicate the nature of his beliefs to his granddaughter, to make her understand. Perhaps even to start the process of passing on those beliefs, those values to her. Christina rejects them utterly, however, the contemporary generational divide revealing itself in the vehemence of her response. "Those damn books", she says, referring to them as if they were fundamentalist texts; which they are in a way. "The books should be burned" she says. They contain poisonous doctrine, fixing beliefs and family mythologies which allow for no revision or reinterpretation in the light of modern knowledge. This is a family fundamentalism, with religious dogma an indivisible component. Christina offers a blunt alternative assessment to Martin's Nosferatu nature: "He's unbalanced... he's mad". Martin hears all of this from his threshold lurking post.

Cuda tells her that Martin's mother took her own life, the family shame too much for her. This is a startling revelation which casts a whole new light on Martin's staging of a suicide tableau at the beginning of the film. Did she perhaps cut her own wrists? Was there perhaps some other cause behind her suicide? Did she feel marginalised like Christina, like Mrs Santini? Whole Freudian vistas are opening up before our eyes. Martin has grown up in a male dominated milieu. As a response, he has favoured female company. Even his sickness is a warped way of finding the close, loving female embrace that was denied him as a child. The Freudian analysis of vampirism—yet another avenue of demystification.

A shot from below positions the open book at the base of the frame, the foundation of the family's traditional outlook—the ancestral storybook. Cuda sounds genuinely heartfelt in his attempts to explain himself, to bridge the generational divide. "People cannot come to other people's beliefs... it is hard for anyone young". There is a cut to Martin at the threshold again, Martin as listener and observer. He has heard all that has been said, and probably not for the first time. He is part of the story and has come to believe in his character, the role he has been assigned within it. Cuda puts forward his side of the argument in the ongoing philosophical struggle between science and superstition, materialism and spirituality which has characterised the post-Enlightenment era. "Do you believe that God's whole world runs by the laws of the few sciences we have been able to discover?" he asks. It's an open-ended question which suggests that the spectrum of man's perception is limited, his knowledge bounded by this limitation. Its natural corollary is the maxim 'there are some things man is not meant to know'; an anti-rationalist, anti-humanist credo. It also suggests that there is still space for magic in the world. Magic and supernatural horror.

Martin is dressed in black, and slips out of the window with feline grace. This is the catlike Martin again. He sits watchfully out on the wide sill, silhouetted under the baleful eye of the moon. He looks like a gothic gargoyle, a creature of the night. It's a beautiful shot, one which would have worked magnificently as a poster image. We still hear Cuda's exposition. Man's materialist rationalism, his lack of faith "makes it easy for Nosteratu — makes it easy for all the devils". Eerie electronic noise blends with the nocturnal cricket stridulation and for a moment we can really see things through Cuda's eyes. The atmospheres conjured up under certain magical circumstances make it easier to believe in the absurd and implausible. Such atmospheres are few and far between in Braddock, however, a place which tends to reduce everything to the level of base reality.

As if to counter this charged moment of magic, the next scene finds Martin in the prosaic surrounds of the kitchen once more, with Christina. The radio talk show babbles away in the background. He's evidently got his way in keeping it on. He insists on doing the washing up, saying "it's my job". He is finding his own place in this female zone, inhabiting it by taking ownership of some of its duties. The affinity with Christina is growing more pronounced. She turns the radio off—she wants direct communication, not the remote confessionals which it is peddling. In the ensuing silence, Martin talks to her. It's the most voluble he's been thus far. "I'm glad you don't believe in the magic" he says to her, returning to his obsessive theme. It's the other side of Cuda's credo, and Christina affirms which side of the divide she falls on with a decisive "well I don't". His subsequent assertion that he is 84 years old undermines this rationalist stance however. He may not believe in magic, in supernatural powers, but he does lay claim to a preternatural longevity which puts him well beyond the bounds of human nature. It's as if he's trying to disappear into the sepia dreaming of the picture album lineage, the history and mythology of which Cuda and presumably his own father have indoctrinated him in. It's a banal supernaturalism. There is no sense that his extended years have been filled with adventure and manifold experiences. He certainly doesn't appear worldly wise. He appears to be just what he is—an introverted 19 year old with a chronic lack of self-esteem. His claim to unnatural longevity is made whilst he is doing the washing up, an everyday chore which counters any glamour or mystery it might generate. This is literal kitchen sink realism. The British new wave of the late 50s and early 60s might even have informed some aspects of **MARTIN**. There are hints of Ken Loach in its naturalistic portrayal of ordinary people in an unglamorous, largely working class environment. I've already made reference to the **KES**-like use of pastoral flute, used during one of the impressionistic sequences of Martin wandering about town. The extensive location shooting offers another parallel with British kitchen sink cinema.

The context in which Martin's implausible claims are made make them less believable. We don't believe them any more than Christina does. She awkwardly attempts to introduce the possibility of his going into a home or hospital, an institution other than the family. She clearly sees the family, this family, as a trap, both for Martin and for herself. She can see the damage it has done to him, but hopes that by getting out he might find his way to sanity and eventually even happiness. It's not a possibility that he's willing to entertain, however. "It would be too hard for me", he says. The family is a trap to the extent that it institutionalises its members. They can't envisage an independent existence beyond its rules and boundaries. Christina says, with the intense frustration of someone who realises they've come up against an insoluble problem, "they're crazy, they're the ones that are..." the unspoken word at the end of the sentence is 'mad', bitten back since its utterance would make it clear that she was thinking of Martin in such terms. She is unaware that he has already heard her talk about him in such terms. This is RD Laing's outlook explicitly stated; the family as an institution which breeds insanity.

Martin is too firmly embedded in the familial institution to even think about leaving however. "I'll be fine", he says with resignation in his voice. "I'm always fine". It's the outlook of someone who's grown used to limited horizons, to merely enduring. He talks as if he's been through it all before, as if these are circumstances he's faced time after time; and as the archetypal outsider cast as monster, perhaps he has. He's just the latest incarnation. His resignation is also a way of downplaying Christina's angry repudiations of the family mythology, the shared delusion. There's a fundamental lack of communication here. It's as if Martin doesn't even hear her. He is as immune to her passionate pleas as Cuda is to his refutations of magical thinking. It is Martin and Cuda who are locked together, an inseparable binary relationship each side of which defines the other.

Christina mutters incomprehensibly, reduced to the state Martin exhibited when he first met her. Speech is eradicated, communication silenced within the family household. She is about to leave when Martin adds, whilst facing away from her, "I'd like to have a phone". This is his manner—to take the conversational initiative just as someone is leaving, so that the exchange will be brief. It's the equivalent of Columbo's "just one more thing", a parting comment which has all the more impact for being added as a seeming afterthought; an addendum which catches the subject off guard. The desire for a phone does indicate a desire to reach out. But as previously noted, it is ironically more likely to have the effect of isolating him, diverting him along paths of remote and disconnected communication. Removing him even further from his authentic self.

Cut to the phone engineers entering the house, desire automatically translated into reality. Christina is evidently someone who gets things done when given the opportunity. Cuda stands at the bottom of the stairs, nodding uncomfortably at the workmen and muttering to himself. His authority has been undermined, and there are now lines of communication out of the house which bypass his scrutiny. The telecommunications equivalent of those rail lines radiating out of town. It is no longer such an enclosed domain. But for Christina, the nature of this communication is unchanged, her arguments with Arthur continuing at a distance. Martin hears her and hides his phone under the pillow, as if it is somehow tainted. He watches through the bannisters, the imprisoning bars, the camera focussing closely on his observing eye. Christina walks back and forth, her legs revealed beneath her short nightshirt, her face concealed. She has become an objectified image to Martin's secretive gaze, the woman he has got to know depersonalised from this lurking perspective (one which we as the audience are complicit in). She is obviously talking to Arthur, at one point shouting "I'm so sick of you". The potential for remote contact provided by the phone extension has further facilitated his evasive inconstancy and made the widening gulf between them all the more pronounced. A new technology supposedly increasing the possibilities of communication has in fact only amplified misunderstandings and disconnections. It will do so later when Martin uses it to call the radio chat show, using it as an open confessional.

A close up of Christina's knees, seen from Martin's bannister viewpoint, cuts directly to a scene on the train. Martin's appetites have been aroused once more. The train is a symbol of these appetites. It is a complex, interlinked symbolism. Martin leaves town on the train to seek the blood which will sate his hunger, obeying Cuda's dictates not to take anyone from the locality. The train is also the escape route from a town which has been bled dry, a dying industrial centre which was once the vital productive heart of a system of national and international trade. Those same railways once carried the steel which was produced in the mills to markets across the country and over the ocean to the world beyond. 'What Braddock makes the world takes' was the proud motto of the town. All fresh blood has now drained away, leaving behind only those locked into their circumscribed orbits, incapable of achieving escape velocity; the old, the poor, the deluded and the insane. And those for whom it has become a commuter town. Martin himself is a commuter of sorts. Acting according to Cuda's dictates, he has to leave town to satisfy his cravings. It's a symbolic commute too, however. Fresh blood and vitality now reside elsewhere.

Martin is in black, perfect for blending into the shadows. It's his creature of the night attire. Sleazy saxophone music accompanies his excursions into the world of Pittsburgh's sex industry, shiftily browsing the racks of sex shops and lingering outside porn theatres. A lewd mechanical toy which sets a couple humping beneath the sheets marries his interest in such toys with the repressed desires which he is seeking to satisfy here. The worlds of childhood and adult toys set into uncomfortable contrast. Martin's hunger is rising again, a physiological change which his donning of black generally signifies. The probability that this hunger is ordinary sexual desire warped and redirected down pathological avenues is made plain by his nocturnal explorations. This would certainly fit in with the critic Robin Wood's Freudian interpretation of 70s new American horror as representing the return of the repressed. Wood tends to view this as an underlying, semi-conscious theme however. With Romero it is absolutely plain and on the surface. There is no need to excavate hidden meanings. The furtive nature of Martin's autodidactic sex-education and the seedy surrounds in which he is obliged to further it is indicative of a society which, for all its much-vaunted 'permissiveness', is still deeply repressive on an everyday level, beyond the hustlers' marketplace. Martin's repressed nature, the ingrowing source of his monstrous appetites, is thus the result of both familial and social forces. His evident lack of experience and knowledge also makes a nonsense of his claim to be 84 years old, and makes it clear that the black and white sequences in which he is beckoned in by willing, sexually available women are fantasies rather than 'memories'.

We cut from the sleazy quarters of night time Pittsburgh to a daylit supermarket car park where a woman is being hustled by a group of young black men as she carries her groceries to her car. Linking in with the previous scenes, we are presented with the other side of the objectification encouraged by the sex industry; a woman who is obliged to run the gauntlet of jeering and whistling attentions in the course of her everyday activities. There is an implied class element to this encounter as well. The car park is a no-man's-land, an interzone between the safe, policed environment of the supermarket's well-stocked hangar and the suburban home to which she will transport her booty. It's the small expanse of the depressed, downtown territory which she has to negotiate, and the hungry jackals are there waiting, seeing what small pickings they can worry from her. The use of a supermarket also spells the downfall of Cuda's business, whose clientele seem mostly older women. The early-middle aged, middle class women buying their groceries here before driving them to their homes on the outskirts of town are a sign of things to come. They will favour the convenience of a one-stop shop where everything is available under one roof. The local grocery store as a social nexus, with its personal service and home deliveries, will soon become a relic of the past. We can't help but think of the shopping mall to which the central quartet of characters in **DAWN OF THE DEAD** retreat (a mall which was located in Monroeville, some 30 miles south of Pittsburgh). And again, Braddock can lay claim to historical and cultural significance in that it was the site of the first A&P supermarket, opened in 1936, a grocery chain which in many ways anticipated the modern developments in corporate food retailing. The supermarket Martin is loitering around is supposedly in Pittsburgh, but the actual store may be this Braddock landmark.

Martin, meanwhile, is blending into the background, dark glasses on (another signifier of the hunger), watching. His introverted character allows him to go unnoticed. He has absorbed the lessons in how to become invisible, magic powers of self-erasure layed out by Kate Bush in her song 'How To Be Invisible' on the 2005 LP Aerial. He mentally notes the address of the woman he has 'chosen' from the cheque which she signs at the checkout — the credit which is still a sign of affluence at this point of history revealing identity and residency. This is an early, pre-digital example of data theft. Martin uses the disconnected communications and remote technologies of the 1970s to gain his 'magical' entry into the home of a stranger.

An ice cream van music box plays a tinkling version of 'Papageno's Song' from *The Magic Flute*, Mozart reduced to mechanised advertising jingle. We are in the suburbs now, the affluent outskirts of Pittsburgh, clean and well-trimmed. Martin is with the children gathered around the van, saying hello to a little baby and buying himself an ice-cream. It is a picture of innocence and he seems very much a part of it, at ease with the kids. It's the first time we've seen any children. Braddock has appeared bereft of them, the place which Arcade Fire sing of in 'City With No Children' from the album *The Suburbs*. The new generation is absent, the town left to the old, decaying into a gerontocratic outpost with no future. Children seem to bring out something vital in Martin, an easeful manner which allows him to interact with people in a natural and outgoing way. But the arrival of the woman from the supermarket at the house opposite makes us realise that he is in fact staking out her place. Nevertheless, a different side of Martin has been revealed. The potential for normality.

Martin appears at the door of the house with a 'help I am deaf' sign held comically upside down. A hint at a wry sense of humour perhaps. He is once more on the threshold, waiting by an opened door. Martin has remained 'dumb' throughout most of the film. He now adds a feigned deafness to render himself even more incommunicado. His appearance results in much middle class embarrassment on the part of the super-market woman and her husband, who appears much more hardline in his attitude, attempting to dismiss Martin's artless charity hustling out of hand. Possibly a little in-joke, for this is a reluctant cameo from Richard Rubin-stein, Romero's business partner. As part of the Romero film-making family, he was co-opted into the role, in the spirit of compadres turning their hand to diverse tasks in order to help the grand endeavour. One for all and all for one and make us a cuppa, would you. His rather offhand, dismissive air suits the character perfectly. The small donation which Martin solicits can perhaps be seen as an invitation of sorts. It also gives him some insight into the nature of the household. Again, there appear to be no children. None of the three women who feature in the main body of the film have children. It's not presented as a failure to fulfil their biolog-ical imperative. But it is a further symbolic representation of the barrenness of the dead surroundings. A place with no children is a place with no life, no vitality. No future.

Martin in night-time black is in catlike mode once more, climbing the wall of the suburban home and spying through the windows beneath the eaves. It is a modern construction, the diametric opposite of Cuda's traditional, slightly run-down wooden house. Repeated minimalist phrases on flute, oboe and electric piano have something of a Bernard Herrmann-esque quality. An acknowledgement of the element of Hitchcockian voyeurism at play here perhaps, a voyeurism in which the audience is complicit (as Hitchcock would frequently make plain).

The next day we see the woman saying goodbye to the husband as he leaves on a business trip, her parting "don't do anything I wouldn't do" a rote homily which actually suggests that both will be doing exactly what the other plans. His patently insincere "you know me better than that" merely affirms it. As he turns to open the automatic garage door, her smile instantly fades, replaced by a look of dismissive contempt. This is another childless marriage in which the husband is frequently absent from the home, leaving an unfulfilled and marginalised wife, excluded from the workforce. Romero's concern for the plight of the traditional housewife in the post-60s world is carried over from **SEASON OF THE WITCH**. It wasn't a particularly fashionable concern in terms of second-wave feminism. But for all his countercultural and socially progressive leanings, Romero has always favoured everywoman and man characters in his writing. He's something of a Springsteen of the movie world in this sense. Martin, as ever, watches all, weighing and assessing. There is an element of the sociologist to him, coolly observing and evaluating. A psychopathic sociologist.

A shadow is cast on the white, slatted façade of the garage door. It is a contemporary **NOSFERATU** (1922) moment, expressionist shadows across the walls of the modernist castle. The 'hunger theme' is introduced, with flanged electric piano, black and white gothic flashback fantasies duly intercut. The echoed and stretched out 'Martin' whispers with female invitation. But Martin has to use modern technological 'magic' to gain entry through the back door, using the remote garage door controller which we've seen him purchase at an electronics store. In the garage, as he begins to half unscrew the lightbulb so that it's illumination won't reveal his presence, we hear the sound of someone approaching. He quickly hides in the car. As the woman opens the door, we have a moment of Hitchcockian tension. Will he be discovered? And why are we holding our breath hoping that he's not. It's reminiscent of scenes in **STRANGERS ON A TRAIN** (1951) and **FRENZY** (1972) in which we find ourselves tensely watching the efforts of the films' villains to recover the evidence which will incriminate them. Hitch uses the mechanics of suspense to make us identify with characters who are murderously psychopathic. We have seen what Martin is capable of at the start of the film and it is clear that he is planning something similar here. Yet we still feel that tension. His single eye peering over the sill of the car's passenger window is a side-wise gaze, a warily catlike scrutiny waiting for the coast to clear. We are reminded of his uneasy presence in Mrs Santini's car, his eagerness to be released from his confines on that occasion.

The woman goes back inside and Martin continues, unscrewing the lightbulb. Three piano notes sound as he enters the house, the notes we've heard as his prelude to breaking into the train compartment. Then there is silence. It's worth going into the following scenes in some detail, since they exemplify Romero's editing skills, his mastery of pacing, rhythm and the build up and release of tension. The house invasion scene in **MARTIN** is really something of a tour de force, a real technical accomplishment (particularly bearing in mind the limited resources available). But this is not empty technique. Its formal qualities perfectly express the thematic concerns of the film. This is the controlled, expertly articulated language of film serving the interests of the story (and certainly not the 'blatant, misfired attempt at a long, battering sequence' which Richard Combs accuses it of being in his Monthly Film Bulletin review). Romero, normally very self-critical of his work, evinces particular pride when talking about this sequence on the DVD commentary for **MARTIN**.

Martin explores the house, padding through with quiet, prowling grace. The black and white chequered bathroom, epitome of ostentatiously eye-popping 70s style, contrasts with the adjoining wood-panel effect living room; the modern and the fake antique existing side by side in a decorative hedging of bets. A cut links the two and highlights the contrast. Martin walks off screen left in the brown room and we cut to the bathroom where he walks onscreen right. It's like a magical appearance, almost in the style of Méliès films from the dawn of cinema. As the bag is place on the basin, the needle filled, the voices increase in intensity. We see one of the gothic Hammer women, laughing and holding a three-branched candelabra as she coquettishly runs away. Martin's dream self, in loose white blouson, the apparel of the romantic hero, follows eagerly, engaging in this playful game of hide and seek. There is a particularly lovely shot of Martin running up a curved staircase, the camera turning around to follow his arcing ascent. Donald Rubinstein's music perfectly matches this moment, a floating, ethereal blend of electric piano and vibraphone.

The chequered wallpaper of this dream realm echoes that of the bathroom. Romero remarks on the happy confluence on the DVD commentary. This was a location which was opened up to them, but as ever, maximum use was made out of what fate provided. Extemporisation spurred creativity and suggested happy visual correlations which could be joined together in the edit. The contrast between the modern house and the gothic dreamworld is particularly pointed in this sequence. Modular shelving in one, statues and urns in the other. In the real world, Martin creeps surreptitiously along the corridor. It's a negative reflection of the dream world, where the chase is a playful game, acknowledged by hunter and 'prey'.

The echoed call ('Maaartin') continues, the need growing more urgent. Martin slowly moves through the living room and we are confronted with the prosaic reality of the modern house: the lounge furniture and the stereo speakers. In the dream world the woman climbs into bed, the endpoint of the playful chase, the place to which she has been leading him. This dream of compliance is contrasted with a cut to Martin bursting into the bedroom of the modern house. The woman is in bed with another man. "Who are you?" Martin asks. The dream is punctured, Martin's romantic fantasy betrayed by the banal reality of suburban infidelity. After a pause, a stunned moment on the part of all parties present, Martin dives and stabs the stranger with the syringe stinger, running out of the room after he has injected his venom. From here onwards, the editing is fast and tight, intensely focussed as it dissects the chaos which engulfs the discrete order of this suburban home; cutting it into its component elements and creating a montage of mounting panic and hysteria contrasted with cool, light-footed evasion, diversion and attack. Martin is like the cat-burglar in 60s caper movies, except that his motives here go well beyond the roguish thievery of such suave anti-heroes.

Martin pauses at the closed bedroom door, another threshold moment. He listens to the frantic, argumentative voices within, syringe fangs in his mouth. It's reminiscent of his unavoidable eavesdropping on the domestic quarrelling of Christina and Arthur. A shot of the black and white dream Martin moving away from a patterned door is intercut with the real Martin in profile backing away, brown teapots on modular shelving providing the visual backdrop. It's a visual echo of the contrast between the brown living room and the chequered bathroom which preceded the invasion of the bedroom; a formal patterning. Martin pauses, gathering his thoughts, needle in hand. A native intelligence is at work here. He is not panicking, not fleeing the scene in a state of mental disarray. He is calculating, plotting his next move. And he appears to have made it, suddenly running off, the camera making an uncharacteristic sweep to capture him dashing down another corridor.

Lewis, the interloping lover, bursts out of the bedroom in a less collected fashion. The woman is framed in the doorway, yelling with the semi-coherence of stunned shock, her state of semi-undress underlying the frantic turmoil of the moment. Martin runs down the stairs and again the camera sweeps around to follow him. There is a cut between a befuddled Lewis and the woman yelling hysterical instructions to him. This is the general pattern of the whole sequence. Martin's control contrasted with the rising hysteria of Lewis and the woman (we never do learn her name). Martin leaves the door open as a bit of misdirection. There is a close up of him cradling the phone extension, syringe fangs in mouth. He has rapidly learned the potentialities of this modern device, just as he has employed the remote control to gain entrance to the suburban castle. The woman's attempts to call for help are automatically dispersed by Martin's garbling of the number. The traditional vampire's mesmeric powers are here trans-muted into an ability to use technology to cast a spell which fogs language and the ability to communicate. The modern vampire has no need for supernatural charms with such devices to hand. It is ironic that it is Christina who has effectively taught him this technique by providing him with a phone extension at home. Her attempt to provide him with a conduit to the outside world has inadvertently provided him with the means to cut communications off in this household.

We have swift cuts between close-ups of the woman on the phone, Lewis shambling around the house and extreme close-ups of the syringe fanged Martin making his obstructive phone extension interventions. These cuts create a real sense of rhythm and action without recourse to camera movement, a kinetic montage created in the editing room. Lewis picks up yet another phone extension as the woman hangs up with her foot (the endless finessing of the conveniences which modern technology provides). Lewis figures out that Martin has been on the other phone, preventing calls from going out. But he falls for his ploy and walks out of the open door. Martin dashes into the hall and locks the door. There is a shot of Lewis' hand against the pane of glass framing the door (this is an exposed modern house with plenty of glass), an impassive, intent and fanged Martin on the other side. The inside.

The music for this sequence is busily percussive, with the disruption of suburban order expressed through woozily wavering cymbal sounds and growling and yawping friction drums. Scurrying piano motifs add a bit of free jazz adrenalin. Martin is back in the bathroom, preparing another shot. There is a close-up on the needle and his concentration-fixed face. The woman, who has been screaming for Lewis, steps fearfully outside the bedroom. She is framed through the open squares of the modular shelving, a perspective which implies a scrutinising point of view. Martin runs up the stairs, with their glass windowed walling. This is the kind of modern house in which large expanses of glass make the lives led within transparent, human aquariums inviting voyeuristic spectatorship. Here, this visibility adds an extra dimension of torment to the nightmare for Lewis and the woman. Lewis sees him running up the stairs from the other side of the glass, and he knows exactly what he's about to do. She sees him too, and retreats back into a cupboard in the bedroom, where she is soon cornered. Romero somehow manages to shoot from above, looking down into the claustrophobic cubicle of the cupboard. Martin opens the connecting doors on either side, effectively penning her in so that he can administer the shot—as if her were a vet corralling a sheep for its injection.

Martin now turns his attentions back to Lewis, who we see wandering in a state of confusion outside, his dazed circling of the house making him appear a little like one of the living dead in Romero's ongoing cycle of films. We see him with his syringe fangs in once more, ready to bite with another dose. He opens the back door and waits in the shadows. Lewis falls for it again, entering only to be immediately subjected to another stab and run attack. Martin runs through the corridor once more. Romero's editing and careful delineation of a relatively constricted space makes the interior of this modern suburban house appear like a bewildering maze, expanding to match the grand staircases and hallways of the black and white dream architecture. The clean modern home becomes a gothic castle in the edit.

The music begins to slow down, to grow lethargic, and the pace of the editing becomes more relaxed as Lewis and the woman succumb to the anaesthetising drowsiness induced by the drugs injected into their bloodstreams. The modern vampire's chemical mesmerism. On the commentary, George Romero cites the influence of his beloved **TALES OF HOFFMANN** (1951), Michael Powell and Emeric Pressburger's highly cinematic adaptation of Jacques Offenbach's light opera. The scene in which two characters duel on barges sets fast action to slow music, he notes, suggesting that he was going for a similar effect here.

As a punctuating gesture to the disorder visited upon the orderly suburban home, Lewis knocks over a lamp and, as he sprawls onto the floor, sends a glass bowl of boiled sweets scattering across the rug. A shot in the bedroom has the phone in sharp foreground focus, the woman blurrily crawling towards it, movement now heavy and effortful. She picks it up, and we cut to a low angle shot taken from below the bed. It's a perspective which emphasises the fact that the simplest act now requires intense concentration. The music stops; events have reached their conclusion. We cut to a close-up of Lewis on the floor, trying to shake himself awake, a blinding circle of light from the fallen lamp beside him providing a cruel, searing illumination. A cut back to a mid-distance shot shows him crawling over the scattered sweets, a painful last attempt at action. Mournful music for oboe and strings accompanies the fading of consciousness, the dying of the light. A cut to the corridor and he is pulling himself along the wall, no longer able to stand unaided. After a cut to the woman, desperately trying to maintain sufficient focus to call the hospital, we see him finally collapse in an ungainly stretch across the bottom of the stairs, reaching up with despairing gesture. The lovers are not to be reunited for a final embrace. As the woman, whom we see in close-up, finally gets through to someone on the other end of the line and tries to articulate a coherent sentence, Martin quietly enters the room behind her and to the rear of the frame, almost an incidental part of the composition. The camera zooms back from her, a movement which expresses her dizziness and disorientation. A cut back to Lewis as he hears a muffled scream, tormented by his inability to reach her, the stairs as insurmountable as a mountain slope. A shot from the bathroom frames him beyond the door, the needle pack in the foreground. He stumbles towards the front door, setting a large picture swinging from its hook, a final element of disorder to end the drama. The motion of the picture is more animated than the barely mobile Lewis at this point, its slicing pendulum swing seeming to mock his final efforts to reach help.

The music stops again. There's a low-angle shot of Martin seen from the woman's crouching perspective as he takes the phone from her and places it back on the hook. He looks grimly purposeful, even a touch admonishing. She has failed to conform to his fantasy scenario, and for a moment Martin appears almost primly puritanical, with the disapproval and moral highhandedness of the romantically betrayed. In the novelisation, the second of two major departures from the tone of the film and the presentation of Martin's character takes place. Martin's anger at the puncturing of his fantasy is directed against the woman. He hits her, and continues to do so in a frenzied rage. 'He looked down at her, panting like a mad dog and foaming at the mouth', Susanna Sparrow writes (and it's worth noting that this is a woman writing). 'He kept hitting her, and she kept coming back for more as if she were a punching bag and he a lightweight boxer practicing for a fight'. It's a passage which is quite explicitly about domestic violence, perhaps reinforcing the idea that Martin might have suffered similar treatment as he was growing up. Despite the rather lurid pulp exposition, there might have been a point being made here about (barely) suppressed male impulses of violence towards women. But it would still have been horribly out of place in the film, particularly given the character of Martin created for (and by) John Amplas. [4]

---

[4] Romero would return to such shocking imagery in his 2000 film **BRUISER**, however. Henry Creedlow, the film's meek protagonist, has Walter Mitty fantasies of a darker, more violent nature. The first involves him punching a female commuter in the face when she pushes in front of him in the queue for the train, causing her to fall under the wheels and meet a gory end. Romero acknowledges the dark, suppressed regions of the human psyche and the likelihood that they will find expression if they remain unrecognised. **BRUISER** is an interesting film to compare with **MARTIN**. In some ways, it's easy to see Henry Creedlow as the sort of person Martin might have grown into had he lived into the 90s and moved with the economic tide. There are certainly thematic connections in terms of the self-effacing nature of the central character and the opposition of real and fantasy selves.

After his admonishing look, it's gentle Martin again, as if he has arrived at an inward decision. "Don't be afraid, you'll just go to sleep", he lulls. "I'm not going to hurt you now because of him", he explains, with more honest than he afforded the woman on the train. "Because of him", he repeats, with a hint of venom. With his romantically chaste view of womanhood, it's the man who receives the censure here. It must have been him who was to blame, who took advantage of her. And it is he who bears the brunt of Martin's angry violence. The psychological necessity of Martin's romantic fantasies becomes apparent when we see his vehement reaction to their undermining.

We cut to an exterior shot in some sort of woodland glade, Lewis's body laid out on an autumnal bed of fallen leaves. It's presumably one of those semi-wild edgelands on the borders of a residential area characterised by scrub and small trees, areas generally emanating a faint aura of incipient menace. Their atmosphere is perfectly captured in the paintings of the artist George Shaw, whose depopulated landscapes depicting the border-lands of the estate on which he grew up in the English Midlands, carry with them the haunted impression of events about to happen or activities which have just been abandoned. Martin leans over the body, a predator looking down on its prey. "You weren't supposed to be there", he says with terse anger. Once more we are aware of the upset which the disruption of his fantasies causes. He picks up a broken-off stick and places it against Lewis' neck, slowly pressing it down until it punctures his throat, the blood welling up and also dribbling out of his mouth. Martin here takes on the role of the vampire hunter, with his miniature stake and sense of puritan-ical righteousness and moral certitude. He has the vampire hunter's denial of the agency of female desire. It is the woman who must be charmed through the vampire's powers of mesmerism. The man must therefore be the interloper in this scenario, the one who has made his forced and unwelcome entry into Martin's romantic fantasy. Martin takes his shirt off to sup from the blood pulsing from the neck, the more traditional locus of vampiric feasting. This is the point where a homoerotic reading might seem apposite. But there doesn't really seem to be any element of desire in Martin's drinking of Lewis' blood. He leaves the body fully clothed for one thing. A mid-distance shot shows Martin in the glade lapping greedily from the body, looking like some woodland beast. This is the vampire in lupine form, pure animal hunger, an urban wolfman. He looks up with the alertness and wariness of a wild creature, blood smeared across his muzzle.

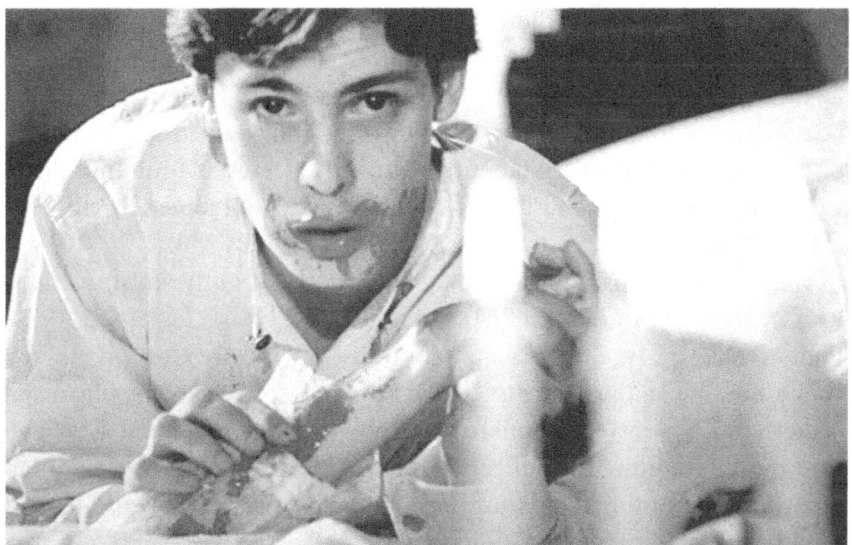

We cut to the black and white fantasy in which he is supping from a woman's wrist, looking up to make the parallel with the woodland feasting apparent. The romantic dream is superimposed over the sordid reality, but the gulf between the two is more apparent than ever. A hissed "Nosferatu", Cuda's curse reiterated with the reverberant dream acoustic of the movie playing out in Martin's head, heralds the hunt for the wild creature. Martin has committed a murder which can in no way be disguised as a suicide. The Van Helsings of the forensics department will see the puncture wound in the neck and possibly the evidence of further tearing and rending and come to a fairly immediate and horrific conclusion. This is the point at which the monster commits an atrocity so great that the previously passive peasantry becomes sufficiently outraged to overcome their natural indigence, take up pitchforks and cudgels, light flaming brands and set off in a rowdy and disorderly mob looking for blood. In his afterword to the novelisation of **MARTIN**, Romero points to the way in which the reaction to the monstrous can be as savage, or even more so, than the behaviours which it seeks to punish and eradicate. 'The mob which pursues the vampire is terrorizing', he writes. 'Armed with the fetishes and weapons of a barbaric horde; outraged that the alien would presume to borrow a bit of human essence for his survival'.

This is also the point where Martin's radio confessional first comes in. The burden of guilt has made him phone the talk show which has so fascinated him in an attempt to explain his nature—the nature of the beast. Perhaps to himself as much as anyone. The guarded wall of silence built up around Martin's taciturn introversion comes tumbling down whilst he is on the phone in talk show. He suddenly unleashes a loquacious torrent of words, casting them out upon the airwaves.

We see a shot of Martin with blood around his mouth whilst the radio host, full of the unrelentingly excitable cheer characteristic of 1970s Radio 1 DJs says "yeah, I've seen that in the movies, people trying to stop your kind". The radio dialogues which punctuate the rest of the film act as a demythologising commentary, voicing the themes that have been running through the film thus far. They also provide an ironic counterpoint to some of the images they accompany. As Martin's Warholian 15 minutes of fame establishes itself, the phone-in show provides a further elucidation of Romero's perennial theme of the failure of communication in the modern world; and particularly in a modern world characterised by increasingly sophisticated technological means of remote communication. There's an inherent sadness to the spectacle of Martin sitting alone in his room pouring out his soul to an inane talk show host who clearly has no interest in anything other than providing sensationalist entertainment, keeping the ratings high to keep the sponsors happy. The evident disconnection between an isolated young person with an urgent need to express himself and a remote, exploitative medium which offers the illusion of intimacy, of a caring auditor, has found innumerable parallels in the growth of reality TV and, of course, in the murky byways of social media.

Romero has highlighted the ambiguous nature of modern media from the outset, with the television broadcasts the inhabitants of the besieged house in **NIGHT OF THE LIVING DEAD** gather around providing more misinformation and conflicting accounts than helpful insights. The analysis from the TV newsroom at the start of **DAWN OF THE DEAD** amounts to little more than a clash of belligerent talking heads, unpalatable truths drowned out by outraged respondents. DIARY OF THE DEAD moves into the internet era by exploring the way in which truth can be edited and manipulated on social media, its currency becoming increasingly devalued. The exploitation of real, vulnerable and sometimes desperate people for the purposes of entertainment is something that seems of particular concern to Romero, however. His 2000 film BRUISER begins with another radio talk show, one in which the tone has been ramped up to a shrill pitch of confrontational rhetoric. One angry caller appears to commit suicide live on air, although he later calls back to reveal that this was a hoax, a way of gaining attention. Truth becomes malleable, easy outrage and violent emotion eclipsing rational analysis and verifiable fact.

The gothic atmosphere of the black and white dream fantasies seems to be growing more pronounced, perhaps in line with the onset of the radio confessional. Despite his efforts at dispelling what he claims to be common misconceptions of the vampire's nature, fed by film and television, the popular image is reinforced. Swathes of dry-ice fog swirl around an old stone building, the walls of a castle perhaps. The mists are parted by a 1930s car gliding slowly and soundlessly past. It's a startling touch which prompts an inner temporal shift. We are not in the 19th century world most commonly associated with gothic vampire tales, but in the first half of the twentieth century. There is a close-up of the statue of an eagle followed by a shot of an angry, torch-wielding mob. The interpolation of car and eagle are particularly interesting here. The car pinpoints a period in time, and the eagle hints at a geographical location. The turul bird, a mythical black eagle, is the national symbol of Hungary, and the two headed eagle was the heraldic emblem of the Austro-Hungarian Empire.

The hunting down of Martin by a violent street mob against such an implied backdrop gains an added historical resonance. The monster as scapegoat could also stand for the scapegoating of the 'other', socially marginal groups or 'outsiders' who become victimised, targeted by populist political movements and the disaffected hordes they martial together in times of economic hardship. Perhaps Romero was thinking of the Hungarian screenwriter Emeric Pressburger, a Jewish man forced to flee one European country after another as the climate of murderous anti-semitism mounted throughout the 1930s, before finally finding a home in Britain, and an artistic partner in Michael Powell. Romero has often expressed his love of the films of Powell and Pressburger, and of **THE TALES OF HOFFMANN** in particular. In any case, the 1930s saw a massive migratory shift in European populations as people fled racial and political persecution. And many ended up emigrating to America, of course. Some ending up in steel towns like Braddock.

This is the longest black and white dream sequence in the film so far. It really does feel like an old movie within the movie. Again, its positioning after the point at which Martin's radio confessional has started seems significant. As the black and white Martin runs alongside a wall, the real Martin pelts down the length of a chain link fence. The parallels between the two worlds, and between contrasting generic forms (gothic horror and social realism) are rigorously maintained. The pursuing figures in the real world are imaginary, the phantoms of guilt and fear. We cut to Martin in the house washing off Lewis's blood and undressing the woman as he lays unconscious on the bed. Romero effects a dramatic contrast in mood between the two scenes. The frantic flight from the mob is followed by a still interlude in which Martin is in complete control once more, his moment of rage spent. He acts slowly and deliberately, the edgy animal wariness left behind. Donald Rubinstein's electric piano, blending with the softly reverberant chimes of the vibraphone, builds up glassy chordal structures, creating a sense of half-awake lethargy, of slightly queasy satia-tion. The radio narration continues in the background, Martin remarking that "it was really hard before the needles". There is something narcotic about these scenes, a slow, drugged haze which has temporarily fogged our perceptions. It's partly a comedown from the kinetic build-up and release of the house invasion sequence. The echoed 'Martin' cries herald feelings of sexual desire, and we see Martin embracing and presumably having sex with the comatose woman, a grotesque counterpoint to the fantasies of smiling Hammer glamour wafting through his fantasies.

The corridors which had been the setting for such frenetic action are now depicted as eerily empty spaces, the violence fading into haunted memory. Martin painstakingly rights the disorder which he has created, setting the picture straight, scooping up the sweets and putting them back in the bowl, standing the lamp back on the lounge table and washing the blood off the doorknobs. All the while, his radio narration voices his feelings with naïve directness, prodded on by encouraging words from the host. He defines himself as an outsider, shut off from normal, everyday discourse and ordinary human relationships. He states Romero's themes of miscommunication, misunderstanding and monastic isolation in the simplest terms: "People are the hardest thing. When I see people together, they don't really talk, not really. They don't say what they mean". Martin casts himself as observer and listener, a role which we've seen him playing throughout. The observer whose perspective we share, through whose quiet gaze we gain an impression of the local society and its inhabitants, its varied strata. There's a pointed irony in Martin's statement about a lack of real communication being made to a radio call-in show, the host of which is treating him with barely disguised contempt—just another weirdo on the wireless.

Martin talks about the "sexy stuff", which he has "been much too shy to ever do". "I mean do it with someone who was awake", he adds. Martin's repression, his uneasiness with the direct use of the word sex, suggests a virginal unworldliness which would surely have been tempered were he really 84 years old, with all those women in nighties beckoning him on. Our sympathies are strangely divided here, an indication of how much we have grown to understand Martin and his conflicted nature since first encountering him preparing for his train assault. He is still a monster, as his admission of doing "sexy stuff" with comatose women as well as drinking blood from the neck of a murdered man attests. But he's also a desperately lonely young man who feels cut off from all human discourse, all ordinary communion. He's a monster who longs to be normal. "Someday maybe I'll get to do it awake, without the blood part". Actually, he's already partway there. Desire and the hunger for blood have already been separated in this instance. He would like to "just do it with somebody, then be together and talk all night". Not just the satisfaction of physical desire, but a genuine emotional connection with another human soul. The boy who hardly ever speaks wants to talk all night. At the moment, the phone extension and radio show are as close as he can get to fulfilling that wish. And that's not close at all—it's a world away.

The last we see of him at the end of this lengthy and formally complex sequence is a glimpse of his face through the jointed slats of the garage door, shot from inside as it rolls shut at the click of his remote control button. It's an anguished face full of unrequited yearning and despairing sadness. There's no real release here. As the garage door slams shut, a modern variant of a portcullis clanking down to guard the entrance to a castle, he disappears from view. He is shut out of this domestic world whose defences he has temporarily breached. Ultimately, his invasion has merely served to underline what he has never had and believes he never will have. In this last image, he is more alone than ever.

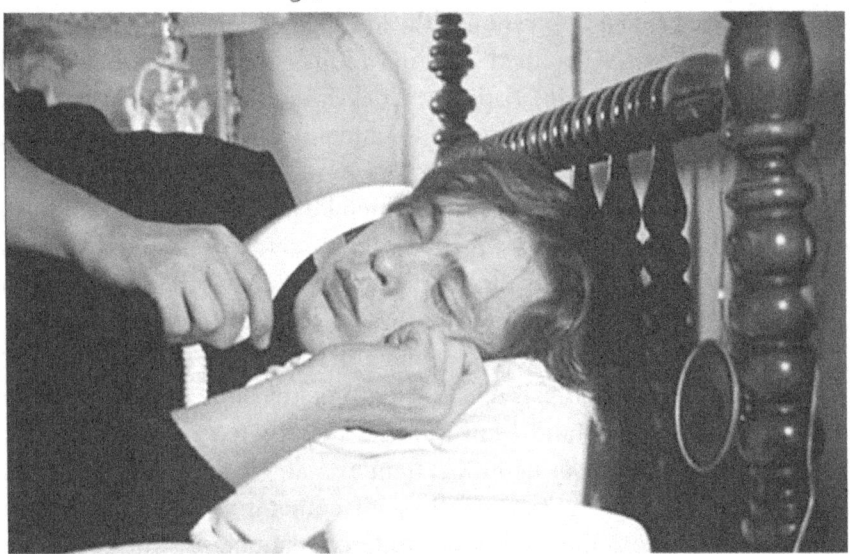

We cut to a shot of Martin lying on his bed with the phone cradled in his hand, still in black, the colour of his nocturnal excursions (his vampire's costume). There is an associational link here with the phone extensions in the previous scene, and the way in which he relieved the woman of the receiver which she was desperately clutching, cutting off her attempts to reach help in the outside world. The bed too reminds us of his embrace of her drugged body; now he has only the phone to hold close. The way in which this scene directly follows on from the image of

Martin looking forlorn and desolate as the mechanical barrier of the garage door locks back into place, leaving him isolated in the darkness, suggests that it is an increasingly unbearable weight of loneliness which has driven him to call in to the show and bare his soul. An element of doubt is also entering his mind, sparked by the unanticipated complications he has just encountered and the troubling challenge to his assumptions and reflexive behaviours which they have given rise to. He feels an urgent need for self-reflection, for an examination of his fundamental nature. Who is he? Why does he do what he does? Why does he find ordinary human communication so hard? These are questions he is asking in an attempt to define his authentic self, and perhaps even to change, to quell his unnatural hunger and find some degree of happiness and acceptance. In the terminology of modern psychology, he is putting himself through a course of cognitive behavioural therapy. There is a delay between the conversation on the phone and the voices as broadcast on the radio which Martin has on in his room. It's a hollow echo which carries a feeling of emptiness, of a dialogue devoid of any real communication. The words thrown back into the confined space of the attic room as he attempts to express himself have a mocking quality, like an inner voice constantly denigrating any positive thought quashing it before it can counter a relentlessly negative self-image.

Martin continues his programme of demythologisation, disspelling the world and replacing magic with realism, supernatural characteristics with rationally described origins. "That's not like in the movies either", he complains, describing the sporadic nature of his hunger, his need. The fact that Martin looks to the movies to provide some kind of authentic truth suggests a failure to recognise their fantastic nature. The dividing line between truth and fiction, the real world and the movies is clearly a thin one in his mind. This line also reveals the extent to which cinematic representations of vampirism have affected his own self image. This dispelling of the world may also be a form of self-exorcism, a dawning awareness of the clear distinction between reality and fantasy. "What else isn't true? Are you going to dispel the other myths?" the host asks, prompting further revelations. "The sun bothers me sometimes", Martin weakly responds. "Night-timers, we're talking to the count", the host announces in his excitable tones, instantly christening Martin with a belittling nickname; the sort of thing which will go down well with the listeners and provide an easy hook for further 'episodes'. "Yes, a real, live honest-to-goodness vampire". The programme cuts to ads. The host is audibly excited as he talks to Martin off-air. He's proved an instant hit and is boosting ratings. As a voice hawks some product which is "now 66 dollars", the connection between ratings and advertising revenue is also made clear. Martin's painful self-revelations, taken as the amusing ravings of a delusional madman, can serve the ultimate purpose of the show: selling more shit. The radio host asks Martin where he can get a hold of him, perhaps thinking of getting him into the studio. Martin immediately puts the phone down. That's not a level of self-revealing intimacy he wants. This is a remote confessional, with anonymity in the Catholic style an essential component allowing for the unrestrained unburdening of the soul.

A cut to a montage of church steeples and towers seems to underline the connection. It also provides a satiric contrast with the announcement immediately preceding, the knockdown sale advertising suggestive of a reaction to economic slowdown followed by the soaring architectural advertising of the church, raising its symbols high and heavenward. As we will discover, the church is suffering a downturn in its fortunes and pros-perity as well. The variety of architectural styles on display, the spires, cupolas and domes with their western Catholic and eastern Orthodox crosses or their pointed avoidance of representative symbolism indicate the divisive schisms within Christianity and its attendant culture, as well as the concentrated diversity of the immigrant population to which they cater — or once did.

In Martin's monastically unadorned room, the camera picks out a small pane of coloured glass in the window, like a piece of stained glass in a side chapel. Martin is a silhouette lying in the foreground, a recumbent tomb sculpture in the chapel. He forms a dark landscape, with headland and shoulder ridge, a geological giant who could have been still for aeons. Cuda walks in, dressed in his white suit, a monochromatic contrast to Martin in black, with all the simplistic symbolism such a duality has long embodied. He turns the light on to find Martin sleeping vampire-style, arms crossed below his head. Or maybe he really is in a recumbent tomb sculpture attitude, a posture preparing for his pre-ordained fate. Cuda shakes him awake, the church bells ringing their mechanical carillons in the background. This also presages the final scene. Cuda orders Martin to church; not to do so would be a 'disgrace' to the family. This is social ritual as much as sacred duty. Cuda is also honouring his pledge to save Martin's soul before destroying him. There is something significant about this simple scene. It feels like the opening of the final chapter, Cuda's forceful and commanding reappearance marking the beginning of the final act. All that follows could be seen as Martin's Passion, in both a sacred and profane sense.

The church is a gutted wreck, an unromantic ruin. The service is held in an attic room, undecorated save for arrangements of ladders and lengths of chipboard leaned against the walls. And here's George Romero himself playing the priest, a nicely understated performance with well-judged moments of lightly mocking humour aimed at the Catholic church in which he was raised back in Brooklyn. He devotes his sermon to the issue of rebuilding the church, a great challenge to one such as he who is "new to the community". The church has evidently been burned out quite recently; Cuda crosses himself ostentatiously as the disaster is referred to, as if it were not accident but the work of demonic forces. But the fact that the congregation fits easily within this temporary space speaks of a more long-term decline. The new priest comes from outside the community. He has been assigned, in effect new blood injected from elsewhere in the absence of fresh local supplies. The elderly rector, to whom Father Howard has deferred in the matter of rebuilding the church, declares that "now is the time to express your faith". And the means of doing this is through raising money. Effectively, it's a fire sale. The parallels between the church and the advertisers hawking their bargain wares on the radio in the preceding scene are made even more apparent.

Mrs Santini sits in the row behind Martin, Cuda, Christina and Arthur, and Cuda sits in between Christina and Arthur. Propriety is observed in the eyes of God, the Catholic church and the local community despite what we actually know about the lack of any true harmony within these family relationships. Again, the lack of children is evident. Romero's priest, Father Howard, is conspicuous by his relative youth. He will be admonished for it later. Mrs Santini leans forward to tap Martin on the shoulder and nod hallo. He nods back. At the end of the service, her husband will pull her away from her attempt to talk to Martin. It's a small gesture which says much about the dynamic of their marriage. It's important to bear Mrs Santini's Catholic faith in mind when we discover her eventual fate. It also adds to her spiritual inertia, her inability to escape from a loveless and childless marriage; a marriage which is barren in every sense. This is the inertia which afflicts the characters in James Joyce's Dubliners stories—The Dead in life (and wouldn't the mature Angelica Huston have been perfect for the role of Mrs Santini). As the parishioners walk out, the organist plays a familiar piece of music; it's **MARTIN**'s theme, given an ecclesiastical arrangement. Its diegetic use here, the soundtrack arising naturalistically from sources within the film's narrative, is playful. But it also subtly makes the connection between Martin's fantasies which it generally accompanies and Cuda's rigid religious beliefs. They are equally delusional, the musical connection hints.

In the street after the service, Martin ambles a few paces behind Cuda, Christina and Arthur, as if adhering to some unspoken hierarchy which has been in place since he stepped off the train onto the platform at Pittsburgh. He does his 'limping' walk, but here it seems much more playful, not occasioned by a heavy burden carried unaided. He seems fairly carefree, increasingly comfortable in the surroundings he has begun to explore and inhabit in his own right. The distance from the family begins to seem more a matter of choice than banishment. He is still as watchful and observant as ever, looking up at the buildings around him. An upward shot looking back at the shell of the church follows his gaze. The old east-facing rose window, designed to catch the rising sun through its stained glass windows now frames the sky. It's a modern version of the gothic ruin, an inelegant hulk set within a rundown urban environment; another refutation of traditional gothic romance. Cuda reveals that he has invited Father Howard to lunch. "You will make supper", he tells Christina, a command rather than a request. More family hierarchies and assumed roles made plain.

An impressionistic shot of rain introduces a change in the weather. The camera focusses in on raindrops teetering on the tips of autumnal blades of grass; or macramé tassels as it turns out. We are back at Mrs Santini's, and Martin is on the threshold once more, fixing her door. She looks longingly at him, a pendant silver crucifix glinting prominently below her neck. A sad James Taylorish song plays on the radio, underlining the wistful mood. She touches his hair, like the old woman to whom he made a delivery earlier in the film. But this is not like someone petting a friendly dog. After all, Mrs Santini has directly made the analogy between Martin and a silent, watchful cat. "You're so gentle, so nice", she says. "I only want to hold you". This tentative expression of feeling, Mrs Santini making herself emotionally vulnerable before him, is too much for Martin. He dashes off, throwing back "the door is finished". Another of his parting statements, this one evidently incorrect. It's not the cross which has driven him away, it's the prospect of intimacy, of emotional and physical connection.

We are present at another family mealtime, but this time Father Howard is at the table as an ameliorative, mediating influence. It soon becomes clear that he's more interested in the wine than any theological matters being discussed. Cuda holds forth, openly criticising Father Howard's predecessor, Father Corelli. He accuses him of leaving of his own volition, betraying the town he was supposed to serve. Father Howard mildly responds that he was forced to leave through ill health, adding that he believes he may have cancer. He crosses himself in a rather perfunctory fashion before popping the olive he'd been holding into his mouth as if it were a self-administered Host. Martin looks on with amusement at Cuda's evident discomfort. A further little sign that he's taking the first steps towards establishing independence from his patriarchal dominance.

The patriarchal order of the house is made evident as Christina serves Cuda and Father Howard sherries in the living room after the meal. She remains there to serve drinks and cookies rather than to take any active part in the conversation, although the Father makes an effort to engage with her at various junctures. Cuda attempts to exert his influence over the new priest, whose comments on the wine and these after dinner drinks make it clear that his concerns tend more toward the corporeal than the spiritual. "This is a town for old persons, Father Howard", Cuda informs him. An old town with old ways requires 'a priest who believes in the old ways'. In fact, we've seen from the rump of the congregation and the ruinous state of the church that the old ways are in danger of dying out. And the absence of a new generation signals the death of the town as well, unless it is to become a commuter satellite town populated by the likes of Mrs Santini and her husband. Braddock's population loss in the wake of the wholesale industrial collapse of the region was dramatic. In a 2008 article in *The Monthly Review*, Braddock's then mayor John Fetterman pointed to a 90% decline in the town's population level since its peak in the 1920s.

Cuda questions the Father about his beliefs concerning demonic possession. This provokes awkward laughter and an embarrassed plea from Christina, before an adjustment of attitude is made to respond to an unsmiling and clearly deadly serious parishioner. Father Zulemas is recommended as someone who "actually does the old ceremony". Cuda nods, repeating the name. Mentally he is evidently already dismissing this young upstart with his lack of regard for the old ways. Zulemas is someone who he can deal with, someone of his own generation. The name even makes him sound like he might come from the old country. He pointedly finishes his drink. Father Howard makes a sly reference to **THE EXOR-CIST** (1973) on the way out. Zulemas had seen it and criticised the portrayal of the rites for their lack of verisimilitude. "I don't suppose you saw that movie?" Father Howard asks, fully knowing the response. "I thought it was great". No doubt, given that it was pro-Catholic in outlook, written by someone who had been educated by Jesuits and intended the story as a loving tribute to his old teachers. Father Howard, relaxing in an armchair with a cigarette and a glass of wine and treating everything with a mild and insouciant manner, is the temperamental opposite of the wracked and tormented priests in **THE EXORCIST**. He's not battling the forces of darkness, just trying to raise church funds and enjoy a good vintage.

We are looking at the old sepia photos again, ancestors fixed in the stiff, corpselike stillness required of Victorian portrait photography. It is Martin looking through the book this time, searching for origins, a sense of self rooted in resemblances detected in these long-dead faces. Glassine electric piano notes hang suspended in the air like dust motes illuminated by shafts of afternoon light. The resonant chiming of an old standing clock, juxtaposed with the faded photos, summons up the weight of time whilst also making the past tangibly present for a brief, charmed interval. Cuda and an elderly man in clerical robes who is evidently Father Zulemas appear at the glass door to the living room where Martin is curled up by the sofa, bent on performing the kind of exorcism which Father Howard found so quaintly amusing. Zulemas is played by Clifford Forrest, Christine's father and Romero's future father-in-law. Another cast member co-opted from the extended circle of local friends and acquaintances. Zulemas and Cuda are framed in the panel, and the shot is tilted at a slight angle. The visual style of the black and white fantasy sequences is beginning to leach into the representation of the real world. The separate realms, always linked by analogous incident, are reaching their closest point of conjunction. The accusatory whisper of "Nosferatu", drenched in its dream echo and hiss, is uttered once more. The black and white Martin is in the bathroom again. He turns around in abrupt reaction to an invading presence. It's an unfolding edit, six separate shots flowering out like pages of a photograph album being rapidly leafed through. He almost becomes one of the images in the book he has been looking at, joining his ancestors in their monochrome world. It's a brief but beautifully achieved sequence, full of poetic resonance. It suggests recurrent experience or a moment long anticipated. The repeated reflex action of a creature living in fear. Recurrent images are intercut with the real world scenes in another feat of rapid-cut editing which manages to remain entirely coherent whilst using techniques which wouldn't look out of place in the experimental cinema of the underground. Indeed, there's a hint of Maya Deren or Kenneth Anger to the style. A stout old lady holds a statue of the Madonna before her; a priest with wire-rimmed spectacles read from a book; another lady has a necklace of garlic bulbs; a tray of holy water is held level and steady; and a man holds out two lit candles in cruciform defence.

These black and white images, their fast-cut rhythms and tilted angles filling them with kinetic dynamism, contrast ironically with the exorcism carried out by Zulemas and Cuda. Zulemas looks particularly frail and elderly, his hands palsied and infirm as he reads out the ritual text in a shaky and uninflected voice, the proceedings interrupted by the occasional cough. Cuda looks purposefully serious, giving it his best Cushing Van Helsing gravitas. He holds two lit candles in cruciform position in the same determined manner as the man in the dreamworld. But here they drip molten wax onto his hands and his grip is infirm. The Latin reading of the black and white scenes is contrasted with Zulemas' extremely prosaic

English reading, which is drained of all drama or sense of occasion. Only the crystalline electric piano, set to maximum echo and phase, conjures the aura of the supernatural presence which they are aiming to tackle. Martin hunkers down by the arm of the sofa to watch the performance, looking more curious than afraid. The major concern here is that Zulemas will collapse before he manages to get to the end of the rites. Perhaps this is why Martin remains. He feels he might have to help get the old man an ambulance. There is more than a hint of parody here, both of THE EXORCIST and of the subsequent cycle of films which treated obscure corners of scripture with po-faced gravity and a conspicuous lack of humour. Max Von Sydow's exorcist Father Merrin proves unable to stand up to the slew of pea-soup vomit and profanity projecting from the 'possessed' child Regan and succumbs to a coronary attack. Father Zulemas looks like he might succumb merely through the effort of standing for more than five minutes. Meanwhile Martin is receiving 'the call' — the echoed cry of 'Martin' drowning out the admonishing whisper of 'Nosferatu'. He leaps up from behind the sofa and runs off. The call may just have been a subconscious way of prompting an escape from the tedium of this sorry display. Cuda looks after him, the candles held loosely in his hands, and shakes his head, as if Martin has let him down; or once more proved his true devilish nature. In fact, what the whole spectacle has demonstrated is the frailty of Cuda's beliefs, the absurdly flimsy framework of fantasy upon which they are based. It's a fantasy quite the equal of Martin's, and potentially equally destructive. The difference is that Martin is beginning to show signs of a willingness and ability to change.

Following on from Cuda's disapproving look, we find him walking home from his shop in the evening. He is shot in the middle distance, a small and vulnerable figure in the dark and deserted back streets. Heavy mist hangs above the ground, gothic atmospherics overplayed to the point of absurdity. Two unresolved piano chords accompany his progress, an 'approaching fate' theme played with pronounced theatricality. Spooky violin is added, thin and shaky with light mockery, as if it were about to burst into laughter. A caped figure slowly appears around the corner from a row of garages, its shadow cast expressionistically before it, Nosferatu-style. Cuda crosses himself and retreats into the playground he was passing by. It's an appropriate stage setting for this childish piece of play-acting. Cuda stumbles and sets the roundabout spinning, its rusty revolutions adding a creaky rhythm to the soundtrack. The handrails cut across the flame, creating a flickering zoetrope effect. It's a nice shot and the low angle from which it's framed adds to the general air of expressionist pastiche, of cinematic parody. The gestures and framing here are all suggestive of silent cinema. They could almost be seen as a parody of Martin's own dream movie: a parody of a pastiche.

Martin appears at the swings, his entrance heralded by a fruity flourish on the violin. He holds his cape up with exaggerated theatricality and bares his implausibly full and gleaming set of fangs. The red lining of the cape is one of the only times we see this primary colour in all its vividness, unless it's in the form of blood. Cuda crouches on the ground, holding his tiny ivory crucifix up, the rosary beads rattling in his shaking hand. He looks diminished and pathetic in his fear. Martin laughs at him. This is a first. And it's a full and hearty laugh at that. He lets out a spooky 'wooo', making the absurdity of this ghost train charade clear. This feels like Martin's mocking response to Cuda's feeble attempt at exorcism; he gives

him the kind of stereotypical, easily identifiable demon he wants. One which has its own traditional wardrobe. Cuda doesn't see the joke. The fixity of his belief is not open to mockery, or to revision. "You ARE the devil" he declares and brings the laughter to an abrupt end with a vicious blow from his walking stick, the heavy head thudding down on his back. It's reminiscent of the death blow dealt by Claude Rains' character upon his lycanthropic son Larry Talbot in **THE WOLF MAN** (1941). This blow carries with it the hint that Cuda may have been a violent or abusive parent. It will be echoed in a later scene with Christine. It may also be the kind of brutal treatment Martin experienced as a child.

This is a blow delivered in reactive anger against a challenge to his authority as much as an attack on demonic power. Martin turns around, seemingly not feeling the force of the blow, and grabs the stick as it's raised to strike him once more. With eyes looking to the right and fangs bared, he momentarily holds a classic vampire pose. We can believe in this instant that he is possessed of the preternatural power and strength of Nosferatu. But then the teeth are spat out, cheap joke store vampire choppers. "It's just a costume", Martin says, his mood now changed into one of pedagogic seriousness. He wipes the pale-face make-up off and shows its smeared traces on his fingers to Cuda. It's the latest in his series of demonstrations of the mechanics behind the surface appearance of magic. The theatrical costumes and make-up taken off to reveal the ordinary humanity beneath the exaggerated character. In his own way, Martin is presenting a realist manifesto. Cuda watches with a look of genuine distress. He needs this monster. He would be utterly bereft without it. In his afterword to the novelisation of **MARTIN**, Romero wonders 'have we conjured up creatures and given them mystical properties so as not to admit that they are actually of our own race? Do we make them extraordinary out of guilt for what we instinctively recall or our own primitive past? Do we need a mythical whipping boy to punish brutally for our primal sins?' Cuda has certainly performed such conjurations. But Martin has the upper hand here. The old, established dynamic in the relationship, with Cuda domineering and commanding, is shifting. Martin is beginning to assert himself. Cuda's look recognises this. He is losing control, the fear through which he maintains it beginning to weaken.

The next scene finds Martin walking by the railway tracks, idle and carefree. Perhaps his confrontation with Cuda has given him a greater sense of freedom. Another shot of the car breaking yard reminds us of the industrial scrapyard the town has become, the beginning of its precipitous decline into rust belt desolation. It's a corollary to the demythologisation of the previous scene. Realism dispelling absurd fantasy. There are more shots of Martin wandering around town, allowing us to see its surroundings through his eyes. More of this sort of verité material would have appeared in the legendary lost cut of **MARTIN**, which ran to two hours and forty five minutes, but which has sadly been lost, almost certainly for good. Romero's original shooting script was long. "I overwrote", he says in the making of documentary included on the special edition DVD. "I had a lot more narrative". Romero was proud of this longer cut. 'I loved the film at the length', he writes in the afterword to the chapter on **MARTIN** in Paul R. Gagne's THE ZOMBIES THAT ATE PITTSBURGH. 'Though I knew it would never be seen'. He talks about the cuts necessary to pare the film down to a more commercially viable length as being the hardest he has ever been obliged to make. He considered them all worthy of inclusion, shot with care and adding thematic substance, local portraiture and character shading to the film. He and Christine kept a black and white print of this cherished version, but it disappeared from the Pittsburgh office at some point. How wonderful if it were to be rediscovered one day, re-emerging as mysteriously as it vanished. That's one 'Director's Cut' I would truly like to see.

Finally, Martin arrives at Mrs Santini's house, and this time he moves beyond the threshold. That he now has the self-confidence to take this step indicates that the confrontation with Cuda was of immense significance for him. He is moving on, away from Cuda's influence.

"You want me for sex, don't you?" he asks of Mrs Santini. No coy references to "sexy stuff" here, just a bald if rather inelegant directness. Martin is being proactive for once, rather than simply reacting to the demands of others. The smile on Mrs Santini's face is all the affirmative response needed. "I decided I'd really like to do it with you", Martin adds, rather unnecessarily. We cut to a scene of them naked in bed, holding each other close. It's a scene of quiet and touching intimacy. The phone rings but she ignores it. No remote half-communication can be allowed to interrupt such direct and whole communion. The ringing of the phone makes the connection with Martin's call-in confessions and makes it clear what a hollow and disconnected form of communication they are.

Afterwards, in the living room, she puts on an LP of reflective piano jazz and lies on the sofa crying. Martin can't comprehend her sadness and makes gauche attempts to understand. The gulf in their experience is all too apparent. She reveals that she can't have children. This is a town for old people, as Cuda said. A city with no children in it, dying with the passing generation. Her barrenness is a symbolic condition of living here. Martin's failure to respond prompts her to say "that's why you're so nice to have around, Martin. You don't have opinions". He does, of course. We've heard him voice them on the radio. But he's expressing them to a remote and indifferent audience who view him as just another crank. There is further failure of communication here.

We cut to Martin eagerly running down the stairs from his attic room, not caring about the busy tinkling of the bells above him, which sound more celebratory as a result. He wants to thank Christina for taking the garlic down from her door. It's another indication of the diminution of Cuda's authority within the household. Martin is freeing himself from that authority by associating himself with a female perspective, trying to see the world through new eyes.

The next scene is a pointed contrast to the previous two, taking us back to a decidedly male environment. Cuda and Arthur are sitting in a bar, Cuda relaxed and smiling, clearly in his element. This may be the legendary Bettie's Corner Café, the Braddock social hub celebrated in Tony Buba's short 1976 film of the same name. Christina has previously told Martin that she's going out tonight. Arthur has evidently been persuaded to spend his time with Cuda instead. He tells him that he's got to get out, and Cuda doesn't dissuade him on this occasion. Talking of Christina, he says "maybe it's good for her never to marry". He drops heavy hints about the family "curse" displayed by Martin, planting the idea in Arthur's head that it may be a genetic inheritance that would be passed on to any children he had with Christina. He is engineering a separation, hoping that Christina will stay to help him when Arthur leaves. It's a deviously manipulative ploy and one which will backfire on him.

Christina waits on the porch and Martin joins her. Once more he allies himself with a female perspective, finding a comfortable place in a female world which is the direct opposite of the male world of the bar we've just been in. He feels for her and hates seeing her so upset. It's quite obvious whose side he's on. He doesn't disguise his dislike of Arthur for the way he is treating her. The chivalrous romanticism which is such a feature of his fantasies here finds a focus in the real world.

In the next scene, it's Christina's turn to confront Cuda. She's heard what he said to Arthur and it's proving to be the final straw. "There is insanity in this family, and you've got it", she tells him. He slaps her, hard. It's a stingingly convincing blow, and when she turns back her cheek is red and raw from the impact. In its own way, it's as convincing a make-up effect as any explicit gore which Tom Savini has brought gushing forth. This is special make up effects in the cause of realism; the reality in this case being that of domestic abuse. Cuda tells her to watch her language. "Shit on your language" she says, her anger now incendiary. Another slap is the result. She bears it. But this is clearly the end, and the expresssion on his face shows that he knows it. The blow resounds back on him, and it is

he who looks stunned. Christina's anger dissipates and she visibly slumps, full of tired resignation, a realisation that she can expect no better than this. He has lost her. "Well, goodbye grandfather Cuda", she says, flat and affectless; the aftermath of the last blow still electrifying the atmosphere. She bitterly reassures him that she and Arthur will not stay together. "Arthur is just my way out". His ploy has worked, but not with the result that he had hoped for. He can't resist having the last word as she turns to leave. "Christina, you are wrong", he says. She no longer has the will or inclination to argue. "Well then, too bad for me" she wearily replies, not even bothering to turn around before walking out. His final declaration seems weak and insubstantial, a final attempt to assert an authority which is rapidly dwindling.

The next we see of Cuda he is alone at the sink. This will be part of his routine now. He can no longer depute domestic chores to the women of the house. This was also Martin's job, of course. The one he insisted on doing in Christina's presence to save her at least some household labour. Perhaps he will be less insistent once she has left. On the day of her departure, she promises Martin that she will stay in touch. But he is more realistic. "No, you'll forget about me" he says, with no trace of self-pity. "People always go away so they can forget where they were". This is said with the voice of experience, the expectation ingrained in someone who has grown up in a fragmented family. We may be gaining some insight into the reason he left Indianapolis. He goes back inside to avoid final awkward goodbyes and watches them drive off. Cuda calls from the other room for him to finish his breakfast. The camera focusses on Martin's pensive face. He realises that they are alone in the house from now on. Some sort of endgame has been set into play.

Any feeling of incipient oppression and claustrophobia is alleviated by a shot of a field of white flowers, summoning up a pastoral mood. A shift of focus and we see Martin's face staring out at us from amidst the flowers. He looks as pensive as he was in the previous scene, as if that expression had been directly transposed here. But these are hardly the flowers of romance or of rural idyll. A reverse shot reveals that Martin is actually staring down at a smoking steel factory on the other side of the winding, muddy river. This is the Edgar Thompson Steel Works on the Monogohela River, Carnegie's founding mill and one of the few still working (indeed, it remains operational to this day). It is a chosen picnic spot for another tryst with Mrs Santini, about as romantic as it gets around here.

In the immediate aftermath of Christina's flight from family and dead end town, the other woman in Martin's life expresses a desire to escape from her self—to take inner flight. "Take away a piece of my brain", she implores. It's fairly clear that she is suffering from depression, its origin a blend of the inherent and the circumstantial. She strokes Martin's hair, her taciturn cat. "Boy, do I wish what you have was catching", she says, assuming a calm contentment on his part which is, of course, far from the truth. "Some people think it is catching", he replies, an example of wryly self-aware humour on his part which has not previously been evident. "In the movies it's catching", he adds. Always the comparison between 'reality' and the movies. "Give it to me, pleas", Mrs Santini says, the vampire's invitation. The camera frames them lying together through the flowers, bird and insect noise providing background ambience. It's the soft-focus pastoral dream of romantic love. But we've seen the reality behind the veil of flowers. The smoking factory, a last functional relic of a dying industrial town.

The romance is further punctured as we find ourselves back in Cuda's shop. The chorus of female harpies who had been waiting outside the shop for Cuda earlier in the film now turn their attentions to Martin. Mrs Bellini directs her venom at him. "You're lazy", she spitefully suggests. People like their whipping dogs, just as they require their monsters. The one for offloading their quotidian frustrations, the other for carrying the burden of their own dark impulses, acting as a focal point for their savagery or to be the sacrificial scapegoat for wider social ills. Martin's radio commentary recommences after this implicit rejection from the community at large. "There's a lot of people I could do it to if I wanted", he observes. The hunger offers scope for violent revenge, for fantasies of power. Martin becomes a voyeur, a stalker following Mrs Bellini through town. He leaves her alone though.

The hunger is going unfed. "I don't know what I'm going to do. I'm getting pretty shaky", he says. He talks about it as if it were an addiction, a physiological need as great as the craving for a narcotic drug. The needles take on a new emblematic resonance in the light of such an analogy. We see Martin hopping across the puddle in Pittsburgh which he crossed in his initial journey with Cuda, limping under the burden of his bag and of his family curse. There's a new lightness to him now though. The associational link made by this repetition of place makes it clear. He is finding himself, gaining in self-confidence. It only remains for the psychotic link between sex and blood to be removed.

More old haunts are revisited, as if he were trying to revive old senses, old hungers. Back at the supermarket, he watches the women running the gauntlet of car park hustlers, the police forcibly removing one of the more aggressive culprits. He hangs about outside the porn cinema again. And he runs the gauntlet himself, in this case that of the neighbourhood biker and his hangers on. His experience parallels that of the women in the car park. Again, Martin is identified with the female world. He hides in the shadows of Cuda's garden, red flowers framing his face, as the neighbourhood youth loudly carouse. His hunger blends with a desire to fit in, to be a part of society and join in with its celebrations (and there is a suggestion that these may be Halloween celebrations, with their house-calling movie mini-monsters). A beer can thrown into the garden is like a grenade, a missile lobbed in from a world away. He watches the biker making out and crushes the can in his hand, the tension in such a gesture readily apparent. He is very much the outsider here, hiding out in his own (or at least Cuda's) garden.

Returning to the interior of the house, we find him back in black, sitting on the windowsill and talking on the phone. Talking to the phone-in host, the only person he ever talks to on the phone. The host makes light of his hunger, warning his listeners to look out because the count's on the prowl. He follows his inane remarks with a foolish Woody Woodpecker giggle, which causes Martin to slam the phone down, perhaps finally perceiving the way he is being portrayed. The giggle echoes mockingly on the radio.

We cut to a scene in which two bums lounge on a trashed sofa in an abandoned warehouse. It's a parody of living room domesticity. They share some potent hooch from a bottle wrapped in brown paper and one of them reads a newspaper. We are back to the base level reality of the scene early on in the film in which Martin runs into a bum in the toilet of the railway station. These are the victims of the economic depression which has devastated the town. Perhaps they once worked in the warehouse where they now take shelter for the night. Or they may be a couple of the many men laid off from closed steel mills, somehow unable to leave town and seek a new start. One of them reads a newspaper, scrutinising the ads for cars. The allure of materialism exerts its glamour even over those with nothing. The car advertising amounts to a taunting reminder of the prosperity which once poured out from the town's steel mills. These shiny symbols of wealth and plenty were once made from materials manufactured here. Now we have seen them crushed and compressed in the car breaking yard, ready to be shipped out and recycled for use elsewhere.

Martin's attack on the two quietly inebriated tramps is swift and brutal. There are no scenes of careful preparation or romantic dream preludes here. Just a sickening attack with a scavenged length of iron pipe. It's not an easy kill either. The tramp on the sofa clings on to life, groaning and feebly attempting to rise no matter how many times Martin hits him. They may have fallen to the absolute bottom of the social scale, but the impulse to live is still strong. Martin mumbles "just go to sleep", his face full of guilt and self-hatred. There's no way that this can be construed as putting someone to sleep, however. They are being battered to death. This is an attack on those most vulnerable in society. Martin has moved on from attacking single women to murdering homeless vagrants. It's no less monstrous. He looks at the blood on his hands. It's another Macbeth moment, reminding us of the stubborn spot of blood he rubbed off from his forehead in the opening scenes on the train. He throws away the pipe in disgust. There's no meticulous cleaning up here. The squalor of the surroundings and the arbitrary nature of Martin's attack contrast markedly with the clinical, highly organised approach we saw him take on the train at the start of the film. There has been a steady progression towards this scene of seedy slaughter. From the carefully contrived setting up of the suicide tableau on the train through the frenzied extemporisation in the face of unexpected complications in the suburban home to the mere brute cracking of skulls. There are no clean needles and steel razors fresh from the packet here either. A piece of broken glass from the bums' broken bottle suffices to cut through the white shirt sleeve covering an arm, blood rapidly dyeing it red. Martin sucks greedily through the material. His desperate supping is little different from the bums drawing from the anaesthetizing teat of their liquor bottle.

There is a repeat of the black and white washing scenes which heralded the peasants' pursuit after the suburban home invasion scene. Martin splashing water onto his face from a wooden bucket. He breaks into a thrift store setting off an alarm, and begins to change from his bloodsoaked clothes. To do this he has to remove his baseball pumps. This quick change routine is conducted in a mad rush, tension created by the intercutting of shots of a police car rushing through the streets. Parallels with the black and white scenes which are also inserted are once more drawn. The flashing red light of the car's beacon becomes the flickering torch flames of the pursuing mob's torches, the ululating wail of the siren and the shop alarm bells the angry shouts of the crowd. The alarm bells and siren, clashing with grating discord, sound out the rising tension of the scene. Martin, having changed, ties the laces of his pumps with fumbling urgency, the motion of the rocking chair which he has set swaying behind him adding to the sense of time running out. There is a direct link back to the scene in the train at the beginning of the film taking place after Martin has set up the suicide tableau and calmly cleared his traces. Then he had laced his pumps up with leisurely care. The pointed contrasting of that scene with this panicked reiteration indicates the care with which the film has been formally constructed. The use of repetition and variation clearly express Romero's themes and mark the development of the narrative and our understanding of and relation to the characters.

Parallel chases in the black and white fantasy and dimly lit night worlds re-emphasise the gulf between romance and reality. As the filmic Martin is chased by torch-wielding peasants, the 'real' version belts down squalid, rubbish-strewn alleys. Running into another deserted warehouse, Martin effectively runs onto an alternative film set. Genres suddenly intersect to bewildering effect. A black man resplendent in a blue silk suit with matching cap confronts him with profanely expressed surprise. He's wandered into the wrong movie, suddenly stumbling upon a scene from a Blaxploitation picture. Both parties seem at a bit of a loss. "He's just a kid", the black man says to his two card-playing compatriots. They are none other than Pat and Tony Buba, more of Romero's film-making family co-opted into filling smaller roles.

We are led to believe we are in some kind of drug lair. This surprise encounter adds another level to the portrait of the dying town. The drug addict is the strung out ghost of poverty, haunting the derelict spaces of post-industrial towns like Braddock. The bums were in a sense old-fashioned traditionalists in their attachment to the bottle. Martin has stumbled upon the future. Braddock would suffer from a crack cocaine epidemic in the early 1980s. We are gaining a preview here. This is another of the seemingly insoluble social ills which the construction of a monster in Martin helps to sublimate and displace. He is a different breed of addict, one who is easier to define, vilify and destroy.

The police who have been pursuing Martin burst in and there is a further outbreak of real, deglamourized gun violence—sudden and unpleasant. Romero's antipathy towards America's gun culture has been repeatedly expressed in his living dead films. At the end of **DAWN OF THE DEAD**, Peter pointedly gives his rifle away to one of the zombies before escaping in the helicopter with Fran, having just contemplated using it on himself. It's a gesture which offers hope for the future, an abandoning of violence.

The soundtrack to this scene of carnage in which the drug dealers and police pick each other off is an oddly animated and jaunty piece of jazz featuring clarinet and violin. There is a close-up of Martin's eyes watching the chaos and death which he has unleashed. A car horn blares unceasingly, a commonplace movie signifier of death in an automobile (it marks the fatalistic denouement of Roman Polanski's **CHINATOWN** (1974), for example). He runs off past the bodies.

Martin washes in the same toilets we saw him pissing in at the start of the film, another example of formal repetition and contrast. There are now two bums in the cubicles, immediately reminding us of the two down and outs Martin has just murdered. The economic situation is not improving, leaving more destitute in the wake of its steady deterioration. One of them is the person he had glanced over his shoulder at the start of the film. Here he is again, still reading the paper whilst taking a leisurely shit. He talks of heading to Mexico. Even the bums are leaving town. The idea of events coming full circle, reaching some natural conclusion, is furthered by a shot of Martin on the train. He traces the etched outlines of flowers on frosted glass, perhaps remembering the picnic with Mrs Santini. We hear his radio narration telling us and the phone-in listeners that he never heard back from Christina. Some time has evidently passed. The wistful tracing of the flowers suggests that he may not have seen Mrs Santini in some time either. He has become preoccupied with his hunger, to the preclusion of his progression towards a 'normal' life.

The next scene is an odd inclusion. Some 'mondo' cinema verité footage of chickens being beheaded. What is this doing here? Are we glimpsing the depths to which Martin might sink to sate his thirst for a blood (or indeed a possible solution to his unnatural hunger)? A subliminal piece of vegetarian propaganda? It's a brutal and bloody insertion, another deromanticising scene. A glimpse of battery farming procedures, it perhaps also alludes to the way people have been treated in this town. Sacrificed according to the merciless dictates of hardline market values. There is a shot of Cuda leaving the poultry factory followed by one of him in his shop. The link between slaughterhouse source and bloodlessly presented product is forcibly made. A shot from above and behind Cuda's delicatessen counter shows the usual crowd of women gathering, preparing for their own carnivorous feasting.

We find Martin continuing his phone call-in confessions and explorations of self. But he is growing increasingly self-conscious. "Are you making fun of me?" he asks at one point, becoming aware of what has been self-evident to us from the beginning. "I don't know what I'm going to do", he says before slamming the phone into its cradle. This outlet for his self-expression will not continue for much longer. Its inherent dissatisfaction is becoming all too apparent.

He enters Mrs Santini's house. "Abbie?" he calls. This is the first time we have heard her first name. It is a powerful moment, like the transition from the formal French 'vous' to the more intimate 'tu'. In this naming, she becomes an individual, not a married attachment to Mr Santini. This individuality is what Joan is reaching towards in Romero's film SEASON OF THE WITCH, whose alternative title, JACK'S WIFE, better expresses its central struggle for independent identity. The implied intimacy is soon lent a tragic dimension, however. Martin hears a subdued echo of 'the call', the 'Martin' invitation. But when he looks into the bathroom, he sees Abbie half-submerged in the bath, the white surfaces of tub and tile smeared with her blood. A razor placed on the side of the bath indicates the method of her suicide, and an empty glass the possible booze-fuelled prompt to the final act. We see Martin's face in tearful close-up, back at the threshold. We have truly come full circle, this genuine suicide mirroring the faked one Martin laid out in the train compartment at the start of the film. It was only after the death of her character that we learned the name of the actress in the gradually revealed credits. It is only after her death that we learn the personal name of Mrs Santini. Abbie, a diminutive of Abigail which denotes further intimacy on Martin's part. A wonky waltz played by a wobbly violin gives an oddly tragicomic slant to the scene. There's certainly nothing elegant about the tableau of Abbie's suicide; no careful arrangement here. The unromantic reality of death is laid bare. Another act of dis-illusionment. The desperation of Abbie's act is made more apparent by our witnessing her presence in the Catholic church earlier in the film, and the crucifix around her neck which affirmed her faith. Her marital infidelity was the first sin in the eyes of the church, no doubt carrying its own burden of guilt. Her suicide was the second, even more grave. Her dead eye staring above the water level (another Marion Crane moment) is the blank stare of one wholly cognisant of her own damnation. Despite such cognisance, life was simply too unbearable.

We hear Martin's denial on the radio—"I didn't do it". It marks a recognition of the fact that he will undoubtedly be accused of doing it, by Cuda

if no-one else. There is also a weight of guilt in the denial. If Abbie's suicide was genuine, the suicide which he faked at the beginning of the film was evidently not. We find Martin back in his room, in the prison of the house. He has retreated to the radio talk-show once more, a definite setback after we sensed that he had become aware of its parasitic nature. He has become self-conscious and fixated on the movies once more too. A bad sign. In the movies "vampires always have ladies", he tells the host. "Well that's wrong too, you don't need all that". He withdraws into his monastic isolation once more, the small window of intimacy and communion having been closed. "In real life, you can't get people to do what you want them to do" he says with evident frustration. The vampire's powers of mesmerism are illusory, as is BF Skinner's science of 'operant conditioning'. Martin's assertion is, if he did but know it, a positive recognition of free will.

The next scene takes Martin back into the world. In footage which was evidently shot on the hoof ("guerrilla film-making"), incorporating a local parade, he joins a marching band processing down the street. He's getting in step with the kids, once more on the road to normality. Here we see the youth of the town. The city does have children, and Martin joins with them. They offer hope for the future, for his future. The reintroduction of his radio voice seems to recognise this. "You get used to things", he says. "you get used to your life. It all gets easier". There is a genuine sense that he is becoming free of his addictions, exorcising the hunger.

But as we see the church steeple pulled into bleary, waking focus, the baleful influence of religious dogma asserting itself once more, it becomes apparent that his growth will be curtailed. We see Cuda's face, tautly set in a visage of hatefulness. He won't let Martin get away from him. Martin wakes. There is a parallel with the scene in which Cuda woke him to go to church — to save his soul. Now he wakes him to destroy him without salvation, the retribution he promised should he contravene his rules. "I warned you, nobody within the town", he snarls. The camera pulls back and we see the stake already in place over Martin's heart. "Nosferatu", he says, as if to justify his act to himself. It was the first word he hissed at Martin when he crossed his threshold, the defining appellation of the monstrous role he would be assigned within the house. Now it is the closing valedictory declaration of his untameable nature, the vindication for murder. Cuda drives the stake in, and blood sprays liberally around, the final Savini effect. There is no crying out, no struggle. It is a perfunctory death, an execution. Red blood stands out against the prevailing white background.

Recorded bells ring out the chorus to Beethoven's 9th symphony, an ironically celebratory carillon which echoes the ice cream van Mozart jingle earlier in the film. An atheist hymn to universal brotherhood and humanist communion is here played in rote, mechanical fashion on programmed bells.

Martin's dead face, still in the repose of sleep, is spotted with blood. We are drawn back to the initial scenes in which he washed the blood from his face in the train bathroom. There is a patch under his hair in almost the exact same spot which he had difficulty rubbing out in the train bathroom scene at the beginning of the film. The ineradicable Macbeth guilt stain. Martin's initial murder, his staging of it as suicide, is not forgiven. In a way this is the retribution for that act. Cuda is his unconscious judge. He kills Martin because he believes that he is responsible for Mrs Sanitini's death. But the fact that her genuine suicide mirrors the faked suicide of the woman in the train compartment gives his death a certain displaced justice. Cuda is oblivious of this, and is murdering him on a false premise. But we can perhaps see that Martin is paying for the clinical indifference with which he covered his traces in that first scene. He didn't get away with it after all.

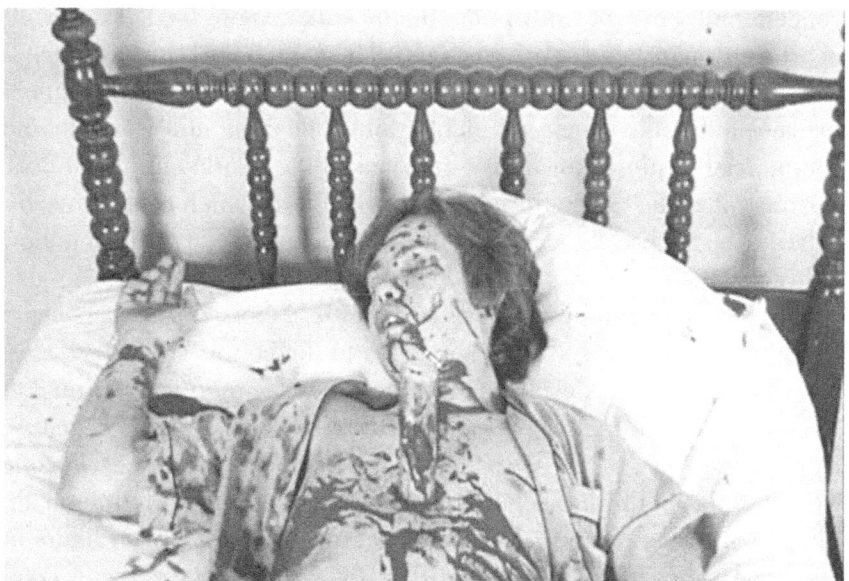

The camera pulls back to give us an overhead shot of Martin lying in bed, the stake jutting out from his heart. Whether he was a vampire or not, this is a deathly impaling. In Paul R. Gagne's THE ZOMBIES THAT ATE PITTSBURGH, Romero suggests that the question of his true nature is unimportant (and this may be the reason he refuses to offer a definitive answer). 'Whether he was born a vampire or whether he was made into a vampire by society at large, it leads to the same result and the same end'. He looks quite peaceful in the repose of death, however. The insipid Beethoven chimes are superceded by the **MARTIN** theme. It's more sad and mournful than ever, with the soprano voice functioning as a funereal lament. There is a shot of the façade of the house; we naturally focus on the window of Martin's attic room at the top. An empty room in a house increasingly haunted by the ghosts of the departed. Then we see a newly dug plot in the garden. This little plot of cultivated land is a diminished remnant of peasant origins in the old world, lives founded upon subsistence farming with attendant superstitions and beliefs. Cuda sows grass seed over what is evidently Martin's grave, kissing his crucifix and placing it upon the soil. He is alone now. This is in some ways his tragedy as much as Martin's. He has talked about the family shame, which must betoken a concomitant sense of family pride. But he is alone now, the last remnants of his family murdered or driven away. All he has left is a business which is failing, about to be driven out by prevailing commercial forces, the supermarkets and malls which will define future retailing and leave the old commercial centres of towns like Braddock full of boarded-up shop fronts. But most of all, he has destroyed the sacred monster which had defined his belief, given a sense of meaning to his life. Martin leaves a spiritual hollow in his place.

Talk-show jabber joins the mournful theme, a cross-current babelogue of contradictory voices. "What happened to the count?" one voice asks. Now that he is dead, Martin can become a mutable monster, all things to all people. An anti-hero to some. "His cloak isn't black", one caller claims. "It's patterned; it's got paisley patterns". A psychedelic vampire. Someone writes a song about him, beginning the process of setting him into myth. Another says that he must be Polish, claiming him as a token figure of identity politics. The host sums it up by saying that "it was a good gimmick". A life reduced to a temporary ratings boosting interlude. Good for advertising. There is one final, tentative voice however (actually the voice of Michael Gornick once more, complete contrast to his animated DJ turn). A voice which, in its very lack of certitude, carries a freight of authenticity. It's a voice which echoes Martin's self-effacing personality. It could even be a voice from Indianapolis, from the veiled past which Martin emerged from. More probably, it is a voice which identifies with Martin's conflicted personality, gentle and at the same time possessed of a psychotic savagery. This quiet voice has the last word. "I think I know who the count is. I have a friend who I think is the count". Monsters breed monsters (and Nosferatu are specifically granted that power). And the need for them is never eradicated. They will always return in some form or another. The Count is dead. Long live the Count.

This bleak ending is really the only way **MARTIN** could have concluded. A film so concerned with demythologisation and with the need to face up to the real rather than retreat into fantasy would have betrayed its own spirit had it offered an ending filled with the illusion of comfort. Martin is a sacred monster and his death at the end is almost like a sacrifice, the end of his Passion in the declining industrial town of Braddock. In his afterword to the novelisation, Romero notes that 'the vampire suits an allegory well, as his characteristics are familiar to us all'. Martin's true nature is really beside the point. 'Man's response to the vampire, to any monster, is perhaps the real heart of the matter. As vile the creature, as brutal man's reaction'. Martin's behaviour, his monstrous appetites may be partly innate, but it is much more likely that they are a creation of familial, social and cultural forces. It is easier to cast him in the old, readily assimilable role of the vampire, with the necessary adjustments to bring him into the modern age. But to do so, as Romero points out, 'is to not only misunderstand him, but to forgive him in a way'. Something of a passive blank slate, Martin takes on the suppressed frustrations and anger of a society whose old certainties—economic, spiritual and cultural—have crumbled away. His murder is a sacrificial offering, the lamb slaughtered to appease a fearsome and unpredictable God. Romero, again in his excellent afterword to the novel, puts Martin forward as being 'an entertainment, drawn in homage to the great vampires we have known, by way of saying: We understand your predicament. You have been created by man, to be punished by man. Your destiny is to be destroyed so that man may be purged'. Of course, this sacrifice achieves nothing. Martin, in his quietly prophetic role, has persistently preached that there is no magic, no supernatural solutions. His realist gospel goes unheard, however.

MARTIN works on so many levels. As a social allegory, a philosophical examination of man's need for monsters, an examination of the pressures of family and community, an impressionistic portrait of a particular environment, an ironic dissection of horror genre archetypes, a psychological study and an overall tone poem. It is perhaps too singular a work to have exerted much of an influence, although its critical reputation and cult stature have grown over the years, since an initially slightly baffled reception. British singer Marc Almond was a fan, and wrote the Soft Cell song 'Martin' in homage to the film, using the dreamworld invocation of the name as a hysterically chanted chorus over Dave Ball's frenetically galloping rhythms. Almond understood the underlying themes of the film too. In the first verse he sings "Martin is a boy with problems/Martin has a family history/Martin has too many nightmares/He lives in a fantasy", going on to suggest that "he's seen too many creepy films". The assertion that he was "growing up in a mining town" is a minor infelicity, but perfectly within the bounds of artistic license (it scans better than 'steel mill town' too). In his autobiography, Almond says 'I thought it highly original' and that 'Dave and I imagined we were writing our own theme song to (the) movie'. He also notes the extra resonance it acquired as the tragedy of the AIDS epidemic took hold in the 1980s. Jim Jarmusch's vampire movie ONLY LOVERS LEFT ALIVE might also be said to show MARTIN's influence, both in its slow-burning tone and its location of one of its modern-day vampires in the decaying urban surrounds of Detroit, which is explored extensively.

Ultimately, though, it is upon an emotional level that MARTIN makes its greatest impact. Romero forces us to care for his monster, even to identify with him (as do the radio listeners heard at the end). This emphasis is immeasurably assisted by John Amplas' hugely empathetic performance and Richard Rubinstein's wonderfully evocative score. And in caring about Martin, we also come to care about the environment we see through his eyes, the declining fortunes of Braddock and its inhabitants. We even come to care for Cuda, his inflexible beliefs and old world values beginning to tremble in the face of the irresistible advance of scientific rationalism and modern market forces (the two not wholly disconnected). At the beginning of this book, I expressed concern that picking apart MARTIN to get at its heart might dissipate its magic. I needn't have worried. Having dug deep into its background, into the history behind its geographical location as well as its production and the details of individual scenes, I now love it more than ever. You see? You see! There is magic...

FILMOGRAPHY

MARTIN—George A. Romero (1976)—(Arrow Films 2 disc version including commentary and documentary)

NIGHT OF THE LIVING DEAD—George A. Romero (1968)

THERE'S ALWAYS VANILLA—George A. Romero (1972)

SEASON OF THE WITCH aka JACK'S WIFE—George A. Romero (1973)

THE CRAZIES—George A. Romero (1973)

DAWN OF THE DEAD—George A. Romero (1979)

KNIGHTRIDERS—George A. Romero (1981)

CREEPSHOW—George A. Romero (1982)

DAY OF THE DEAD—George A. Romero (1985)

BRUISER - George A. Romero (2000)

LAND OF THE DEAD - George A. Romero (2005)

DIARY OF THE DEAD - George A. Romero (2007)

SURVIVAL OF THE DEAD - George A. Romero (2009)

LAST HOUSE ON THE LEFT—Wes Craven (1972)

THE HILLS HAVE EYES - Wes Craven (1977)

THE TEXAS CHAINSAW MASSACRE—Tobe Hooper (1974)

THE AMERICAN NIGHTMARE—Adam Simon (2000)

DOCUMENT OF THE DEAD—Roy Frumkes (1985)

BIBLIOGRAPHY

THE ZOMBIES THAT ATE PITTSBURGH: THE FILMS OF GEORGE A. ROMERO by Paul R. Gagne (1987)

THE CINEMA OF GEORGE A. ROMERO: KNIGHT OF THE LIVING DEAD by Tony Williams (2003)

THE AMERICAN NIGHTMARE: ESSAYS ON THE HORROR FILM eds. Robin Wood and Richard Lippe, including 'THE HORROR OF MARTIN' by Richard Lippe (1979)

MARTIN by Susanna Sparrow and George Romero (1978 Futura paperback novelisation)

Joint review of COMMUNION AND MARTIN by Tom Milne (*Sight and Sound* 1977)

Review of MARTIN by Richard Combs (*Monthly Film Bulletin*, Jan. 1977)

SPEAKING OF THE DEAD—AN INTERVIEW WITH GEORGE A. ROMERO by Lee Karr (2009, on the homepageofthedead website)

NIGHT OF THE LIVING DEAD by Ben Hervey (*BFI Classics*, 2008)

Interview with George A. Romero by James Blackford (*Sight and Sound*, February 2014)

NIGHTMARE MOVIES by Kim Newman (revised and updated 2011 edition)

HORROR: THE AURUM FILM ENCYCLOPEDIA ed. Phil Hardy (1996 paperback edition)

HOLLYWOOD FROM VIETNAM TO REAGAN by Robin Wood, including THE AMERICAN NIGHTMARE AND NORMALITY AND MONSTERS (1986)

MEMORIES OF OVERDEVELOPMENT by Mary Ellen Schoonmaker (article on Tony Buba) in *American Film* magazine (October 1985)

BRADDOCK, PENNSYLVANIA: OUT OF THE FURNACE AND INTO THE FIRE by Jim Straub and Bret Liebendorfer (*Monthly Review* 2008)

THE DOUBLE LIFE OF LINCOLN MAAZEL by Lynne Conner (*Pittsburgh Post-Gazette*, Jan. 2002)

VAMPYRES: LORD BYRON TO COUNT DRACULA by Christopher Frayling (1991)

THE ORIGINS OF DRACULA by Clive Leatherdale (1987)

THE ELEMENT ENCYCLOPEDIA OF VAMPIRES: AN A-Z OF THE UNDEAD by Theresa Cheung (2009)

A TERRIBLE BEAUTY: A HISTORY OF THE PEOPLE AND IDEAS THAT SHAPED THE MODERN MIND by Peter Watson (2000)

MICHAEL POWELL by James Howard (1996)

NICK DRAKE THE BIOGRAPHY by Patrick Humphries (1997)

About the Author

JEZ WINSHIP IS A WRITER, PHOTOGRAPHER, Storyteller, Librarian and member of The Folklore Tapes Collective. A radio presenter for Exeter's Phonic FM, you can find him online at his blog Sparks In Electric Jelly, writing about Film, Art, Music, Literature and myriad other subjects that capture the attention of his magpie mind. His essay 'Quatermass: Rebirth & Ressurection' appears in the forthcoming collection, WE ARE THE MARTIANS: THE LEGACY OF NIGEL KNEALE, while future projects include another entry for the Midnight Movie Monographs series—this time about Czech Fairytale Horror VALERIE & HER WEEK OF WONDERS. When not writing, he can generally be found exploring the folklore and history of Devon, and taking pictures of crows.

This series is dedicated to the memory of Mike Sutton, one of the finest film writers I knew. He was part of this series from the beginning, but sadly passed away before his book saw completion.

Here's to you, Mike. "One of us!"